Uncle Walter's Secret

by

Will Fenn

First published 2017

PUBLISHED IN THE UNITED KINGDOM BY:

Diesel Publishing
2, The Tithe Barn
High Street
Hawkesbury Upton
Badminton
South Gloucestershire GL9 1AY

www. dieselpublishing.co.uk

The right of Will Fenn to be identified as the Author of this work has been asserted by him in accordance with the Copyrights, Designs and Patents Act 1988.

All rights reserved. No part of this book may be reprinted or reproduced or utilized in any form or by any electronic, mechanical or other means, now known or hereafter invented, including photocopying and recording, or in any information storage or retrieval system, without the permission in writing from the Publishers.

British Library Cataloguing in Publication Data.

A catalogue record for this book is available from the British Library.

© William Fairney 2017

ISBN 978-1535596008

AUTHOR'S NOTE

This work was inspired by a brief conversation with the father of a friend, who showed me the medals that he had been awarded by the Polish Government in Exile whilst he was a member of the SOE.

The work is totally fictional but based on real events and some names have been changed accordingly.

Given their ability to readily read the German ciphers, were the Allies really taken unawares by the counter-attack through the Ardennes Forest 1n 1944?

Cover picture
THEY LANDED BY MOONLIGHT by Robert Taylor
© The Military Gallery
www.militarygallery.com

Prologue

10 Downing Street
Whitehall

2nd April 1946.

Mr T.P.Sexton
321 Townsend Road
Chesham
Buckinghamshire

Dear Mr Sexton,

The Prime Minister has asked me to inform you, in strict confidence, that he has in mind, on the occasion of forthcoming list of Birthday Honours to submit your name to the King with a recommendation that His Majesty may be graciously pleased to approve that you be appointed an officer of the Order of the British Empire.
He would be grateful if you could inform him within the next two weeks if you are graciously prepared to accept such an honour.
Please treat this letter in the utmost confidence and reply to me directly at Number Ten Downing Street.

        Yours faithfully

D.P.T.Jay
Private Secretary

When the last of the mourners had left, the two daughters started sorting out his possessions. Amongst them they came across a battered old box file and inside they found a large number of letters and other papers, a large collection of stamps and first day cover envelopes and a pile of identification papers and aliases:-

El Lobo

Raymundo Garcia

John Rollings

Milok Toporek

Clam

Patrice Lefebre

Kurt Pfeiffer

There was also a small glass-fronted display case containing a 1944 German unaddressed First Day Cover envelope with an elegant stamp showing a beautiful white racehorse and a white foal. In German, the stamp was headed 'The Brown Riband of Germany, 1944'.

The women also found two faded leather boxes. Inside them they discovered splendid medals and insignia, clearly never worn.

The Commander's Cross with Star of the Virtuti Militari.

The Polonia Restituta.

The highest Military and Civilian awards that can be made by the Polish Government.

Chapter 1

Recall

The new Prime Minister's voice crackled out of the fretwork cutouts in the ancient Pye wireless.

"Having received His Majesty's commission I have formed an administration of men and women of every party and almost every point of view. We have differed and quarrelled in the past, but now one bond unites us all: to wage war until victory is won, and never to surrender ourselves to servitude and shame, whatever the cost may be."

"Turn it off, Reggie." commanded a resigned voice from a deep armchair in the opposite corner of the room.

Reginald Hawthorne, tall and gangly, loped swiftly across the room and snapped off the set. "So," he said, "the die is well and truly cast. We have been thoroughly skewered. Now it must be Plan B."

From the armchair the lazy voice emerged through a cloud of grey smoke "You know damn well Reggie, there is no Plan B. Winston has been playing a long game. Over ten years long. He's run rings round Eddie Halifax and now Plan A, if there ever was a truly thought out plan A, is well and truly dead."

"I'm totally lost Sir Cedric," an exasperated Frederick Younge in the opposite corner queried, "what on earth is Plan A when it's at home?"

"Sue for peace, of course!" fumed Sir Cedric Attenby from the armchair.

"and now, with the Nazis swarming all over the Low Countries, Winston has made that impossible, at least at the moment. He has too much of the country roused and supporting him."

"Eddie will try again soon," opined Hawthorne, "but I don't hold out much hope. Winston will just move him on. He only kept him in his new Cabinet as a show of unity. 'Keep your friends close, but keep your enemies closer' is Winston's mantra. That will end if Eddie or anyone else for that matter shows signs of going soft. Meanwhile Winston is implementing his own Plan B. Total all-out war. We have got to work out the ramifications and see how it affects our operations. I can't believe that no-one had foreseen this. Espionage in time of war is entirely different to peacetime and so we are going to have to change up several gears and recruit more agents. That's your department Freddie."

"It won't be easy," Younge replied, dismayed. "BP has already mopped up the best brains in Oxbridge."

Hawthorne shrugged. "That's not really the problem. Bletchley Park needs the swots, but we need operators, an entirely different kettle of fish. It shouldn't be a problem. Military, or even criminal types are what we need, but you will have to move fast, get them before they all get called up, so you can train them in our methods."

Sir Cedric had been quietly listening in his own little cloud of smoke. Knighted just a few months earlier for 'Services to the Intelligence Community, and for Charitable Works.' He and his wife ran a re-habilitation home for 'Fallen Women', usually unmarried mothers. Rumours amongst Sir Cedric's staff suggested that he had been involved as much in the 'Fall' of several women, as well as the 'Rehabilitation', but they were, after all, only rumours.

Attenby's rise through the intelligence community had been slow and steady. Not for him the spectacular revelation of another state's secrets or the assassination of enemy spies.

No, his career took off during the First World War when he was a junior attaché in Palestine. The Balfour Declaration, whilst acclaimed as a triumph of diplomacy in Europe, had caused major disruption and riots amongst the indigenous populations of Palestine. Attenby's ministrations had placated much of the unrest but a simmering undertone of disquiet remained. Nevertheless his name had cropped up more and more in diplomatic circles and his career began a rapid rise. Because of his contacts in the Jewish communities he had been directed to lead undercover activities in Eastern Europe in the early 1930s as Hitler rose to power.

His approach was through a combination of diplomacy and recruitment of traitors in the enemy camps. By sheer hard work and intellect he had built up a picture of the thinking at the heart of most European countries. Attenby had warned previous administrations of the dangers to Czechoslovakia and Poland and was well aware of the ingrained defeatism at the heart of the French government and in parts of the British cabinet.

Now the Head of Allied Intelligence Liaison, in his office eight floors above Baker Street served by an unreliable lift, was thinking out a new strategy. His body was kept fit by the need once or twice a week to climb those eight flights of stairs when the lift was faulty, but his mind was kept agile by the extreme challenges of the job.

He was already thinking further ahead.

"What about instructors? Will we have enough? Can we pull one or two back out of the field? Surely with northern Europe rapidly being over-run, we need to secure our networks pretty damn quick."

"Not so easy," said Reggie, "with the situation so fluid, we need all the intelligence we can get. Boniface is working miracles, but there's nothing like a pair of eyes on the ground."

Freddie's ears perked up. "Boniface, who's he?" Sir Cedric let out a huge "Hrrumph!" And spluttered "Nothing, no-one to worry about. Just an agent in France. Forget any mention of him."

Freddie was sensible enough not to press his question.

Boniface was the topmost secret of British intelligence. It was known to only to a handful of men in the War Cabinet and intelligence services on a highly secret List. Even Winston Churchill, when he was appointed by Chamberlain as First Lord of the Admiralty at the outbreak of war in 1939, was not fully briefed. Some Wehrmacht cyphers had been broken, but not Navy or Luftwaffe ones. It was only after being made Prime Minister on the previous day that Churchill had been briefed about Boniface in full.

With its highly secret information about German army movements, Boniface was derived from the breaking of cyphers created on Enigma coding machines. The cyphers had been first broken by Polish intelligence officers in 1932, but the secret was not passed to British intelligence until the outbreak of war in 1939. A unit to crack the cyphers had been established in the grounds of a stately home in Buckinghamshire, Bletchley Park, 'The Park', or 'BP' as it was affectionately called by all involved. Attenby, as head of intelligence liaison between the Allies, and Reginald Hawthorne his adjutant, were on the List. Freddie Younge, however, despite being head of Polish liaison, was not. He of course knew about Enigma, but not that it had been cracked and was providing the high quality Boniface information which emanated from it.

"We need every contact we have in France at the moment," mused Sir Cedric, "With the high mobility of the German Panzer Divisions, we must know where they are heading."

"Well if we can't use France, what about Poland?" said Reggie.

Freddie began to realise why he had been called to this meeting. "We're now getting some high quality results from our network in Poland," he replied defensively. "It'd be a shame to put that all in jeopardy." Sir Cedric concurred with this. "I know all about your network and its good work. You're quite right, we don't want to upset that. But what about "Clam?"

Reggie suddenly saw the way it was all going. "Ah!" he said. "Clam? What about Clam?" He thought a moment then added "Yes, I see what you mean. His work's just about done. We could pull him out now. It's taken him ten months to set up the network, but it virtually runs itself now. He trained those agents for the circuits and he could train lots more back here. Mind you, persuading him to do so would be another matter. He loves working with those Poles you know, and he's a very independent guy. You know what the Irish are like!"

"He'll do what he's bloody well told, Irish or not! Pull him back!" Attenby bellowed.

After Freddie had left Sir Cedric said "You really must be careful about Boniface Reggie, careless talk and all that. I know Freddie's trustworthy, but if he's not on the List, then he's not on the List."

Reggie gazed out of the window across Baker Street to the sandbags in front of the buildings. "Yes, I'm sorry Cedric. Freddie's as sharp as they come and he'll pick up on anything. If we send him out into the field at any time, we can't afford for him to give anything away if he's caught."

Freddie Younge had recently returned from the Moscow Embassy and was full of useful information about the debacle of the German-Russian non-aggression pact which had caused the Poles, British and French so much by angst when it was announced. His main finding was that the Russians had been taken completely by surprise when approached by Joachim von Ribbentrop the German Foreign Minister. Stalin, normally of a highly suspicious nature, had seized Hitler's offer of a pact with both hands. Attenby was trying to figure out why. Perhaps Stalin had his own agenda.

Freddie had maintained close contact with his Polish opposite numbers whilst in Moscow until Russia had followed Hitler's lead and invaded Poland from the east to complete a pincer movement.. He had been instrumental in the break-up of the Russian network of agents inside the country. His new job now was to establish relationships with agents inside Poland itself.

Chapter 2
El Lobo

Terence Patrick Sexton was born in August 1920, in Chesham, Buckinghamshire, to a Catholic family. His father Valentine was English and had just been de-mobbed after serving as a signals officer in the Great War. His mother Margaret was of Irish stock from a long-established family of Mullingar in West Neath. She insisted that the birth be registered in Ireland and so a week after he was born she took Terry on the ferry from Fishguard to Dublin.

The sea crossing was very rough with a sullen sky and sharp vicious squalls. The baby cried all the time and Margaret took him above deck to avoid the looks of the other passengers in the cramped smoke-laden lounge. Her nerves were in tatters and she nearly threw him overboard several times. When the boat at last docked she took a taxi to the family farm, a good two-hour journey.

Terry was christened in the little village church, then having spent the first six months of his life with his maternal family, Margaret took him back home to Chesham. His father's wartime experience had given him the skills necessary to apply for the job of the town's postmaster and he was duly appointed. Terry's earliest memories were of being taught Morse code and receiving telegraph messages on the brass and Bakelite keyboard in the back office of the Post Office in the centre of Chesham. His father then paid him a few pence to deliver them around the streets of the town.

From the age of three Terry started collecting stamps. As well as his buying stamps from the post office, customers would bring in stamps for him and soon he had a collection from all around the world. For his fourth birthday Valentine bought him a first day cover envelope and stamp for the British Empire Exhibition, and from then onwards Terry collected every first day cover that was issued, continuing well into adulthood.

For Terry's tenth birthday Valentine bought him a crystal radio set. Terry had to string a long copper wire out of his bedroom window and across the garden to act as an aerial. He would spend many hours with Rich, his best friend from school, listening to tinny reception from local and distant radio stations, sharing the headphones back and forth. Rich's father was a French teacher at Chesham Bois School and his mother was a primary school teacher at a school in Amersham. Rich had naturally benefited from this academic background and was already saying that he wanted to teach when he grew up.

One day in 1932 Rich came round to see Terry at home, bearing a magazine that he had bought. 'Practical Wireless' had an article about how to construct your own two-valve radio and Rich had decided to spend his pocket money on buying the components. Terry did the same but it was several months before they had gathered together enough parts to start making the sets. It was a completely new experience to have amplified sound coming out of a loudspeaker and he made himself very unpopular with his parents when the scratchy atmospherics filled the house.

Every summer Terry's mother would take him to Ireland for several months to stay with his grandparents. They owned a dairy farm that spread over rolling pastures running down to a tranquil lough. There were a large number of aunts and uncles in the area, nearly all farmers or foresters. Raised a devout Catholic, Terry was fluent in Gaelic from these frequent visits. He loved the rich green countryside and spent many hours exploring the thick woods around his grandparents' farm and swimming in the lough. One of his forester uncles, Conroy, taught Terry woods craft and survival techniques and they would camp out during the warmer nights and fish and hunt wild hogs during the day.

The boy showed a strong aptitude for mimicry and languages, learning French and German at school in Chesham. He was fascinated by history and took a great interest in the Napoleonic Wars. His time spent in Ireland together with talking with his mother at home resulted in him speaking with a gentle Irish brogue that he alternated with an exaggerated Home Counties accent to impress his school friends.

One day when he was about fourteen, he had knocked on a house door to deliver a telegram and there was no response. He peered through the letterbox to be greeted with the sight of a beautiful naked girl standing in the hallway at the foot of the stairs. He knew from school that she was Vivien, one of twin girls who lived at the house. This first surprise acquaintance soon developed into a strong friendship as he got to know Vivien and her sister Margery well. Very soon they became a close-knit group and Terry, Rich, Vivien and Margery went everywhere as a foursome.

Using their radios Terry and Rich were fascinated to tune in to transmissions from all across Europe. With his grasp for languages Terry found that he could understand much of what was said, and followed the developments in Nazi Germany with great interest. Having suffered a little from racism at school owing to his Irish connections he was particularly appalled by the racist rantings of Adolf Hitler.

Terry was always fiddling with his radio sets trying to improve reception and one night he had disconnected the tuning condenser to renew a soldered joint. He was taken aback when out of the speaker came an American voice, surging in and out of the background static. He thought at first that there must be a local broadcast with an American announcer, when yet another American voice interjected. As he listened Terry realised that this was a conversation between two radio hams in America. From the conversation he deduced that one of them was in Milwaukee and the other in California. He thought that he must have inadvertently retuned his set to short-wave transmissions and that these were radio waves that had bounced their way off the upper atmosphere all the way across the Atlantic Ocean.

Being a regular subscriber to 'Practical Wireless' he knew about high frequency wave transmissions and within a week he had built himself a short-wave wireless transmitter-receiver set and joined into intermittent conversations from all around the world, learning the jargon and techniques for communicating through this very weather-dependent medium.

When Terry was just fourteen he got a job labouring with a construction company. His sharp intellect was noticed and he soon moved into the contracting department as a clerk, and then as a salesman. His work often took him to Ireland and gave him the opportunity to see his family more frequently. During his regular visits he was shocked by the evolving economic conditions in the country. Eamon de Valera's attempt to abandon free trade in 1933 lead to economic collapse and he turned to nationalisation as a way out. Terry's grandparents had to sell their farm and buy a smallholding that barely enabled them to survive. When a mob lead by Catholic priests attacked Connolly House in Dublin, the home of a workers' rights group, Terry abandoned his Catholic faith and joined the Communist Party of Ireland. Because of his linguistic skills he became secretary of the Party in West Ireland. During the mid-1930s they sent him to several Communist Internationales in Moscow, Warsaw and other East European cities. There he acquired a smattering of Russian, and several other languages, in particular, Polish, in which he became very fluent.

Despite Terry's best efforts he could not persuade Rich to go along with his political ideas. Rich was of the opinion that what took place in Europe was not British business and he was fast becoming pacifist in his views. When the Spanish Civil War broke out in 1936, Terry, at the age of just sixteen, was one of the first to volunteer to go and fight with the International Brigades. In defying his parents he caused a family rift which was not healed for several years. Terry tried to persuade Rich to go with him to Spain but Rich was by then fully committed to the pacifist cause and was also hoping to go to teacher training college. He had drifted away from Margery who was now going out with another man from Berkhamstead. Terry and Rich agreed to try and stay in touch by short-wave radio.

Terry gave notice to his employer who was genuinely sorry to see him leave and promised him a job when and if he returned. Vivien was surprisingly unconcerned by his plan and she supported his belief in the rightness of the Republican cause. Terry sweetened the pill when he asked her to marry him. She accepted straight away and he gave her an engagement ring which he had already bought, in the certain knowledge that she would agree. In November 1936 Terry Sexton left for Spain.

There was little training on joining the Republican army. Recruits and volunteers were checked out by CRIM, the organisation responsible for recruitment and training. Terry was given basic drill and rifle training and introduced to hand-to-hand combat. This was considered vital as weapons were in short supply. Training went on for three weeks then he was sent to his unit.

He joined the Dabrowski Battalion lead by Stanislaw Ulanowski. This was one of the first Polish groups to form up and was the first to join the field of battle. It comprised mainly of Poles from the French coal mines in Northern France and Belgium, but also had a smattering of British, Russian and Dutch communists and left-wingers. Terry was particularly fond of the Poles whose sense of humour matched well with his Irish blarney.

Further training took place in a desultory way and Terry learnt to kill by knife, garrotte, bayonet and using his bare hands. Being fluent in many languages and radio work he was eventually assigned to the communications division and made a sergeant in charge of a radio transceiver platoon, reporting to another English volunteer in the battalion, Jimmy Tranter, or 'Sandcastle' as he was called.

Terry was only about five foot six tall, with a thin, wiry body. However, he had an incongruously large, round head, with a long prominent nose and pointed ears like a pixie, that stuck out at either side and so he was given the nickname 'El Lobo', or simply 'Lobo', meaning 'Wolf'.

Over the months in Spain he would become very fond of a cheap Spanish brandy, Veterano and could easily drink a bottle a day yet still maintain his acute mind and sharp wit. The Veterano took its toll however, and his face and nose took on a bright purple hue.

Terry quickly became disenchanted with his communist colleagues. They were a very crude and undisciplined bunch. Whilst Terry learnt the art of killing, often swiftly and silently, this was in fair combat in pursuance of the war. The communists had no qualms however about killing defenceless prisoners of war merely for entertainment.

One afternoon his battalion were resting on the outskirts of a village and came under attack from nationalist forces. The Republicans counter-attacked and were starting to get the upper hand when a squadron of bombers attacked the village and totally destroyed it, killing many of the civilian villagers, mainly women and children. The bombers were clearly German Heinkels although crudely over-painted in Spanish Nationalist colours. His battalion was forced to retreat, but took a number of Nationalist prisoners with them.

When they had re-established their camp a group of Russians from the battalion took the prisoners off into the gully of dried-up river bed. Incensed by the slaughter of the villagers the Russians set about bayoneting the helpless prisoners in the guts so as to prolong their agony as they took several hours to die. Lobo was so sickened by this that he tore up his Communist Party membership card.

He witnessed first-hand the bombing of many more defenceless Spanish villages by German bombers and realised the sickness of the whole Nazi and fascist regimes. \the more he saw of the atrocities by both sides of the war, the more he longed for thr security of home and in his short time in Spain he came to think that democracy, with all its imperfections, was the only true way for members of the human race to live together.

Chapter 3
Valencia

At first the civil war went well for the Republicans and Terry found his unit steadily advancing as the Nationalists retreated. As each new front line developed he established his communications base a few hundred yards to the rear. Orders would be received from the central command post over the radio but instructions were sent to the front line over hastily-laid ground wires. These were frequently broken by enemy shellfire or by troops tripping over them as they could not always be buried.

As the war developed the Nationalists began to drive back the Republican troops. Better weapons, air cover and intelligence enabled them to overcome resistance. Terry's unit were in Catalonia but gradually retreated as the war dragged into 1938.

In March he was relocated to a headquarters communications centre in Valencia where he was set to work with a team responsible for coding and decoding messages. His work also included trying to decode the Nationalist transmissions but these were seemingly impossible to crack.

One day in October 1938 during a particularly hard fought struggle between the Nationalists and the Dabrowski Battalion on the River Ebro, Terry and his team were ordered to take their weapons and join the front line. The Republican armies were suffering serious defeats and a last-ditch attempt was made to pull in anyone fit enough to fight. Both sides had dug deep trenches and carried out successive assaults by going over the top in the time-honoured fashion. It was as if nothing had been learnt from the Great War. It took only two days for the ammunition to run out and then Terry experienced the most horrific hand-to-hand fighting that he would ever encounter. When the Nationalists overrun his trench he managed to survive by killing with his bayonet then with his bare hands, but the battalion was gradually forced to retreat. Once the new defensive line had been established Terry's team were ordered to set up the new communications centre.

A day or two later Terry was brought a strange looking device which had been captured from a Nationalist trench. It was an Enigma machine. He had heard of these machines which had been invented by a German engineer in the 1920s, and sold commercially during the early 1930s. It enabled messages to be encyphered using an unbreakable coding system. It used three wheels mounted in a box with a keyboard, all connected electrically together. Each wheel had twenty-six contacts on one face and the same number of contacts on the other face. The contacts were connected together by a nest of internal wiring. A fourth fixed wheel acted as a reflector of the signals and this ensured that the messages could be decoded.

By tapping the letter keys, current passed through the wiring within the wheels and lit up a lamp which showed the encoded letter. When the next key was pressed, one or more rotors rotated and so the new encoded letter was obtained via a completely different path. Thus if the same key was pressed repeatedly, a different encoded letter was produced each time. When the encoded letters were fed back into a similar machine at the receiving end, because of the reflector wheel, as if by magic, the original message emerged.

The secret of the machine was that the rotors at both stations had to be set up in the same starting position. If an interceptor tried to feed the coded message into the machine, unless he had these starting positions available, garbage would emerge. As there were over seventeen thousand starting positions, and there were other settings that could also be changed, there was no practicable way to break the code.

Thus the machine that had been brought to Terry was by no means unheard of in the communications community. Because of his radio ham work before the war, Jimmy Tranter had been put in charge of all communications, including Terry's team. He had actually used Enigma machines back in England where he had worked for a large bank where the machines were used for commercial transactions. Now he was trying to decode Nationalist messages made with Spanish versions of the Enigma. Jimmy noticed something odd about Terry's machine. As well as the usual rotors, keyboard and lamps, it also had an unusual plugboard on the front, rather like in a telephone switchboard, only smaller.

Jimmy and Terry went to the Battalion commander Ulanowski with the Enigma and told him about the additions to the commercial version. As the writing on the machine was in German, it seemed clear that this machine was not a commercial machine, but one made especially for the German army, and supplied to the Spanish Nationalists under Franco. Ulanowski pondered over the machine, and was perplexed as to what, if anything, to do. Jimmy felt that this was an important development and should be examined by cryptographers, but the Republican forces had no such capability. During his banking days Jimmy had talked to British intelligence officers about Enigma security and felt that the British should become involved. Ulanowski agreed and Jimmy volunteered to get the machine to England via Gibraltar. However Ulanowski said "Sandcastle, we need you here, Lobo, you will have to take it. I'll make sure you have all the necessary clearances."

Terry travelled swiftly across the Republican-held territory from Valencia to Almeira. Passing through numerous Republican checkpoints with his precious cargo, the papers signed by Ulanowski gave him free passage. However the coastal route to Gibraltar from Almeira had been taken by Franco's armies. He discarded his identity papers and disguised himself as a Spanish peasant, Raymundo Garcia, which was not difficult owing to his already rustic appearance.

His biggest problem was disguising the Enigma machine, so he put together large strings of onions and slung them over the handlebars and crossbar of an old bicycle. He hid the Enigma in a sack of onions and strapped it to the crossbar underneath a mass of onion strings. The loaded bicycle was too unwieldy to ride so he spent four days pushing it cross-country from Almeira to Algeciras, avoiding both Nationalist and Republican patrols. His biggest problem was that he was accosted time after time by peasants wanting to buy his onions. He put them off by saying that he had a contract to deliver them in Algeciras but they were very persistent as hunger was rife owing to the civil war. Each time he was able to put them off but received much abuse in return. By the time he arrived in Algeciras his blistered feet and his weatherbeaten face were an ideal disguise. The town was teeming with traders, police, soldiers and spies, but he melded in without difficulty.

Algeciras was only a short distance from Gibraltar but tight security prevented him entering the small outpost of the British Empire. Terry contemplated just walking up to the border and announcing that he wanted to speak to the officer in charge but knew that he would have to pass through the Spanish checkpoint first. He just could not risk being searched. He decided that the only way to get to Gibraltar was by boat.

The promenade above the beaches had guard posts and searchlight emplacements every few hundred yards and the guards patrolled continuously, but did not prevent access to the beaches. Terry casually pushed the loaded bicycle up and down the strip of seashore. he inspected moored boats and fishing vessels, but the armed guards discouraged close scrutiny and the larger vessels had individual guards. The fishermen repairing their nets or unloading their catch were too numerous for Lobo to risk taking a boat in daylight so he decided to wait until dark. Moving around the coast to the east he reached the village of Campamento where the Nationalist army had set up a high fence and a guard post to prevent any access to the road to Gibraltar. Staying well clear of the guarded zone Lobo came across some sails laid out to dry. Waiting until no-one was watching, he quickly cut a section from one of the sails. He wrapped the Enigma in the waterproof sailcloth, making sure that plenty of air was trapped inside it and hid it under the skeleton of a wrecked fishing boat.

Terry pushed the cycle back to a small group of waterfront shops where he was able to sell his cargo of onions to a greedy greengrocer. He was given a mere trifle of what they were worth, but Terry was glad to be free of the load. To avoid looking conspicuous, he rode back to the beach area and left the bicycle against a breakwater. Free of its encumbrance he strolled down to the waters' edge and sat down to bathe his blistered feet. The salt water stung his blisters but eventually the pain eased so he limped back to the breakwater and lounged casually until it started to get dark. He used the time to note that a powerful speed-boat from Gibraltar was patrolling the shoreline of the Rock. It started at the territorial boundary with Algeciras, headed south past the airfield and round the southern tip and disappeared. About fifteen minutes later it reappeared, having, presumably, patrolled the eastern coastline of the Rock. This pattern was repeated several times.

It was a beautiful balmy evening with only high noctilucent cloud which went through the colour range of pale blue, light salmon pink and eventually dark crimson as the sun sank beneath the horizon. The promenade was crowded with people enjoying the evening but as the darkness set in, they mostly headed for the bars

Night fell very suddenly but when it did, the shoreline was raked with searchlight beams from the Spanish promenades.

Terry realised that even now it was not going to be possible to steal a boat without being seen. Ever resourceful he realised that the only way to get to Gibraltar undetected was to swim. As he had spent his youth swimming in Irish loughs this was not a problem, but the question was how to avoid the guards whilst carrying the Enigma. He also had the problem of keeping it dry. Waiting until the nearest guard was at the far end of his patrol and the searchlight beams were pointing away from him, he retrieved the package from beneath the skeleton of the wrecked fishing boat and re-wrapped it in several more layers of sailcloth. Concealed from view by the wreck he stripped to his undershorts and tied the Enigma package around his waist with some fisherman's rope. He had to wait patiently for the guard and searchlight beams to be out of view then slipped into the warm water. The trapped air in the package mercifully ensured that it floated so he was able to strike out for the western end of the runway of the Gibraltar airstrip. He timed his journey to coincide with the eastern patrol of the power boat.

There was a strong current, but it seemed to favour him. Every time a searchlight beam swept towards him, he dived beneath the surface. When he was just a few hundred yards from the shore he dived once more as a beam approached. He surfaced once it had passed, only to see it hesitate and then return. He dived once more and the beam paused, lighting up the package floating just above his head. Suddenly the sound of a machine gun barked out and bullets sprayed the water above him. A few hit the package and many more zinged in the water ahead of him, but Terry was not hit. The package lost its buoyancy and sank beneath the surface and the machine gun stopped firing. The searchlight beam hovered for a few more seconds, then moved on. Terry's lungs were by now bursting so he broke the surface and took deep breaths. He hoped that the gunners had just seen the package as a bit of flotsam.

The Enigma package was now waterlogged and very heavy, but he set off once more for the edge of the Gibraltar airstrip. As it loomed larger, his speed seemed to increase. He realised that the current was taking him past the end of the runway, and to compound matters, the patrol boat reappeared from the tip of the Rock. Striking frantically he gradually made headway towards the airstrip, and eventually felt smooth rocks beneath his tortured feet.

Scrambling to get ashore, he was suddenly caught in the searchlight beam of the patrol boat, which immediately swerved towards him. A megaphone voice boomed out from the boat, ordering him in Spanish and English to stop, but he carried on climbing. Just as he clambered over the edge of the runway and onto the concrete of the aircraft turning circle, a machine gun let rip from the nearing patrol boat. Shot at for the second time in half an hour, Terry flattened himself onto the runway as bullets crashed into the embankment below him, or passed just over his head.

In the distance he heard sirens wailing and the sound of approaching vehicles. As they drew near the machine gun stopped firing and Lobo rose to his feet and raised his arms above his head.

Chapter 4
Sexton

Terry had been fitted with a drab prison overall which was a size too big for him and he looked a very incongruous figure. David Roster, Chief Intelligence Officer at Gibraltar Airbase, was bemused by the man in front of him. His interrogation had elucidated that the man was born in England, registered in Ireland, and with a fiancée and home in Buckinghamshire. He had been found with a bullet-ridden German cypher machine captured in Spain, and had just arrived in Gibraltar after a two mile swim.

Was he a spy or a crank, an agent or even a double-agent? Ireland was a neutral country, but currently embroiled in an economic war with Great Britain. Was this a back-door attempt to steal trade secrets? The sensible thing for Roster was to take advice, so he encoded a preliminary report and sent it to London. Within an hour he had his reply. Sexton, as he called himself, was to be cautioned, charged with espionage and sent under close escort back to England. In addition the Enigma was to be photographed from all angles and the undeveloped film sent on the same aircraft as Sexton. The machine was to be sent also, but London insisted it should travel on a different aircraft.

That evening Terry had an unexpected visitor in the form of the Governor of Gibraltar Sir Edmund Ironside. He questioned Terry at length, going over again most of the ground covered by Roster. He was particularly interested in

Terry's dual nationality and questioned him closely about his views on Irish nationalism and British sovereignty. As a precaution he read out relevant sections of the Official Secrets Act and then got Terry to sign it.

The following morning Sexton was hand-cuffed and loaded with two armed guards onto an Armstrong Whitworth Ensign aircraft of No, 24 Squadron. The aircraft captain was given a sealed portfolio containing a slim report and the film roll of photographs of the Enigma machine. He had strict instructions as to whom it should be delivered when he got back to England.

Taking off from Gibraltar in the early morning sun was a challenge as the light wind was from the east and the rising sun was directly in the pilot's eyes. However as soon as it was airborne the aircraft turned through a half circle and headed due west. Only when it was comfortably on course were Terry's handcuffs released and thankfully he massaged his numb wrists back to life.

With war raging in Spain and German bomber aircraft raiding its cities, the flight was routed around the southern coast of Spain and then the Algarve. Terry peered through the small observation window as they flew over the coast of England's oldest ally. Portugal had been a friendly country for over six hundred years but was a neutral in this war so the flight had to remain outside its airspace. As the aircraft turned north off the most westerly point in Europe, the lighthouse of Cape St Vincent, Terry mused about the great battle that had been fought here. The young captain Nelson had captured, almost single-handed, the Spanish flag ship the San Joseph and received the officers' surrender by taking their swords as the Spanish admiral lay dying from his wounds.

Once clear of the north Spanish coast the Ensign crossed the Bay of Biscay, flew well clear of the Isle of Ushant then on directly towards London. Because of the long detour it did not arrive until late evening, but a delegation was patiently waiting to greet it at Northolt.

Two sturdy military policemen boarded the aircraft and took Terry into custody, handcuffing him again, whilst a shadowy figure in a grey suit and a greyer cloud of smoke held back until the flight crew descended. Stepping forward, Cedric Attenby approached the captain and said "I believe you have something for me?" The captain unperturbed, asked for some identification and Cedric produced a thin document. Whatever was on it had the desired effect and the captain handed over the slim portfolio as if it were red hot.

Terry and his escort climbed into a military van with barred windows whilst Cedric Attenby sank into the rear seat of a sinister-looking low-slung black car. They set off in a convoy towards London.

The first port of call was a heavily-guarded safe house in Acton. Terry was given a room, a selection of clothing and an unusual and ineffective Bakelite electric razor. There were no sharp metal items of any description in his room, and an armed guard outside. There was a sliding peephole on the door and he wondered, with some amusement, if he was considered a suicide risk.

He had been told that a meal was waiting downstairs and so after he had washed and shaved he was escorted down to the dining room where a hot trolley contained a selection of dishes. He was joined by a civilian who introduced himself as Mr Brown, but Terry knew this was not his real name. The conversation over the meal was pleasant enough but he knew that it was really a subtle interrogation. He spoke freely as he had nothing to hide. He merely wanted to deliver the Enigma, spend some time at home, marry Vivien and then get back to Spain.

However that was not to be. As Mr Brown, or Reggie Hawthorne as he really was, learnt more about Terry's exploits, an idea formed in his head. In particular Terry's relationship with the Poles and his linguistic and telegraphic capabilities impressed him. At the end of the meal he politely bade Terry goodnight and said that they would meet again in the morning. Having barely slept for the last forty-eight hours, Terry was only too glad to fall into his bed and a deep sleep.

Chapter 5
Clam

Hawthorne wasted no time and rang Cedric Attenby at home. He agreed to meet him there and buzzed his driver to come round to the front door.

Attenby lived in a large detached house in Eastcote, in West London. It had a long sweeping drive so that late night visitors did not disturb the neighbours who might ask unwelcome questions.

Reggie quickly de-briefed Cedric about his conversation with Sexton and explained his thinking. Could Sexton be persuaded to become an agent and work for British Intelligence in Eastern Europe?

Attenby was scathing. "The man is an Irishman. A communist. He speaks Russian. He's bought an old shot-up Enigma machine and is trying to peddle himself! He's probably a German agent, or a double agent for the Russians! He fails every filter test we have for recruiting agents! I would be a laughing stock if I even contemplated it."

Reggie tried again to persuade him. "Don't you see! Those are the very reasons we should get him! A disillusioned communist is far better than a mercenary agent. With his linguistic skills he could pass anywhere. We started running checks on him as soon as he arrived in Gibraltar. All he's said so far checks out. We've more information on him coming in first thing tomorrow. The Enigma is at BP and their first reactions are incredulous. They say that the machine is badly affected by bullets and seawater but it is being dried out. Most of the critical contacts are brass so they will polish up easily. Because of the bullet damage it won't be usable but that doesn't matter, the wiring connections can be traced. They say that the new plugboard is genuine, and very worrying. They've had hints of it in breaks of other codes and think it may be introduced soon. We're struggling really hard to break Enigma. As it is, we may never break it in twenty years. With this plugboard it could take a century. But at least we have it! We can make a start. No intelligence service, German or Russian, would send us this, just to sell us a double agent! Sexton must be genuine!"

Attenby was not convinced. "This decision's bigger than us. We need to wait for more information, and then speak to the Minister. We'll meet again tomorrow in my office."

Father Constance Molloy took the narrow stone path from the side door of his little house towards the church, as he had done twice every morning for over forty years. His first walk that morning had been in the six-o-clock darkness, but he had needed no lamp, for his feet knew the way intimately. Like the bare patches of a rabbit run, his route was marked with areas of earth pounded hard from years of use, interspersed with clumps of weed where his feet rarely touched. Over these last few years his pace had gradually shortened and the clumps became less distinct. Once or twice he had stumbled when his open-toed sandals had caught in the grass.

It had been many years since he had seen any congregation attend early morning prayer but he still knelt at the altar and recited the liturgy as if the tiny church was filled to the brim with the faithful. Population decline and a growing cynicism with religion had taken its toll.

Now, as he set out for the first Mass of the day, his eyes blinked in the strong sunlight and he felt its growing strength on his face. Mass always attracted a few from the surrounding farms and villages, but rarely anyone younger than sixty years of age. As he entered the churchyard he saw a young man kneeling in front of an ivy-covered tombstone. At first Father Con thought he must be praying, but then he realised that the man was peeling away the ivy to read the inscription. "God be with you this fine morning!" the priest greeted.

"And top of the morning to you Father," said the stranger, "And wouldn't it be the finest yet!"

"Welcome to Saint Saviour's. You must be new to these parts. Will you be joining us for Mass?"

"I will indeed Father, and yes, I'm here looking for traces of my ancestors. You must be Father Molloy. Perhaps you can help me afterwards."

"Call me Father Con. That's the grave of old Valentine O'Leary you're looking at. I buried him there, it must have been these thirty years ago. His family still farm hereabouts. Are you related?"

"Yes, in a manner of speaking, I'm Sean O'Leary, a distant cousin, I'm thinking. I believe I have a second cousin Terry Sexton living here".

"Terry? Yes indeed. I fine man of principal, but he's not here now. He's fighting in Spain, but he writes to me regularly. But come in to Mass Sean, and we'll talk later."

In Cedric's Baker Street office the next day Hawthorne had much more information. Through agents in the Irish Communist Party he had learnt that Terry Sexton had indeed resigned from the Party and had lodged a report about what he considered to be war crimes by communists in Spain. From Polish contacts it had been revealed that Sexton had also made many Polish friends whilst visiting Eastern Europe and was highly thought of by them.

Hawthorne's staff had also done a thorough job of checking up on Sexton's life in England and Ireland. He found that Terry had worked hard in his short time in business and had acquired a high reputation for honesty and fairness amongst customers. No one had a bad word for him.

His priest also confirmed Terry's integrity. He had been profoundly disappointed when Terry left the church, but understood the reasons and said that the Church itself was to blame for fomenting riots. A year ago he had received a letter from Terry. It was just a short note apologising for his lapse and asking forgiveness. It enclosed a torn up Communist Party membership card. They still kept in touch.

BP had reported that the Enigma machine contained rotors specially designed for Spain. They were not the same as those used by the Wehrmacht. This was an advantage because despite the bullet damage, by plotting the wiring of the rotors they would gain further insight into the thinking of the Enigma designers. They were working out the wiring of the new plugboard, but were very sanguine as to how useful it would be. If the Spanish rotors were wired differently to the German ones, the chances were that the plugboards would be wired differently too. A bullet had been retrieved from the mechanism and had been examined. It was of Spanish origin and so Sexton's story was consistent.

Cedric had not slept much overnight, pondering the conundrum presented by Terry Sexton. This new information however made up his mind and he asked for an immediate meeting with the Minister.

Incredibly, the Minister, whilst being aware of the Enigma, was not cleared to know about Boniface and so Cedric and Reggie had to skirt around the issue, and concentrated on Sexton's unique linguistic and telegraphic skills and Polish contacts.

"Minister, he is ideal for Section Nine. Gambier-Parry has been agitating for all new agents to be skilled at W/T, and is even thinking about making it a requirement. This man is ideal for the job." said Cedric.

The Minister frowned. "But Section Nine hasn't even been approved yet. And even when it is, there's no guarantee that Parry's idea will be accepted. The pool for recruiting agents is small enough without restricting it further. It would not look good to start Section Nine off with an Irish communist".

"But Minister, he is only half Irish, has lived in England all of his life, apart from two years in the Spanish Civil War where he was in front-line combat, mostly hand-to-hand. All our checks show that he is fiercely patriotic, and gave up his

Communist Party membership over a year ago in disgust at atrocities in Spain."

"How do we know that this isn't all an elaborate ruse? Could this plug thing just be a plant to mislead us? The Germans are hand in glove with the Spaniards, look at the bombers used on Guernica. This could be linked to a German attempt to subvert Ireland by planting an Irish agent"

"Of course you're right Minister, but we have thought carefully about that possibility. We believe that the balance of probability is weighted strongly in favour of Sexton being genuine".

And thus Cedric pressed hard for approval to approach Terry and see if he could be persuaded to join British Intelligence. The Minister was more worried about the Irish connection than the communist history, but eventually gave his agreement. "But I want him closely watched."

Terry was brought to Cedric's Baker Street office later that morning and the proposition was put to him. He was asked, first of all, to sign the Official Secrets Act. He laughed at this because he had already done so two days earlier when he was cautioned in the presence of the Governor of Gibraltar. "A fine Intelligence Service that doesn't even know who has signed the Official Secrets Act!" He did not endear himself with this. However he agreed to sign again in the presence of Cedric Attenby, as Ironside's report had not mentioned that he had been read the Act and so they had no proof of what he had told them.

Terry was then told that they believed that he had a high regard for the British and asked bluntly if he would be prepared to join the Polish Section of the British Intelligence Service. To their surprise, and a little suspicion, he readily agreed. He was asked why he was so keen to do so and he explained that what he had seen of German and communist atrocities in Spain had convinced him of the vile nature of Fascism. He was very much in sympathy with the Poles whose country was being pressed on both sides by the autocratic regimes of Germany and Russia.

Terry was then introduced to Freddie Younge and told that he would report to him. The first thing for Terry to do was to undergo extensive training. Cedric told Freddie to take Terry away and start an initial briefing, but "First," he said, "we must give you a code name."

"I already have one," said Terry, 'El Lobo', and he explained why. After some chuckling Cedric explained "We can't give you a Spanish name, so we'll call you 'Lobster.'" "Not possible," interjected Reggie, "we already have a Lobster in France." This caused even more hilarity, but eventually it was agreed that Terry's new code name would be 'Clam.'

Chapter 6
Ashridge

'Clam' was initially recruited into the Army as Sergeant Terrence Sexton as his cover and to enable him to integrate back into the English community. As Christmas was fast approaching he was granted immediate leave, with orders to report to the army training centre at Ashridge on 2nd January 1939.

Vivien was overjoyed to see him. He had been away in Spain for well over two years. Terry was still only nineteen and Vivien eighteen and so he asked her parent's permission to marry her. They were initially shocked at the suddenness of the request, but not really surprised. After all, the young couple had known each other for most of their teenage years and had been engaged for over two years. Her parents' real concern was about Terry going back to Spain, where the Republicans were fast losing the war. When he told them that he was to go into the British Army they relented and somewhat reluctantly agreed to the marriage.

The evening was dull with a fine mist of drizzle as Terry rode up to his parents' home, full of apprehension. He need not have worried however as time was a great healer. As he parked his bicycle the front door opened and his mother rushed out to hug him. She hardly recognised him a he had grown so much in height and build. As they went indoors Valentine came to greet him and he too was pleased to see him. Still hugging his mother, he told them about his intention to marry Valerie. His parents had always liked her so were pleased for them both and asked eagerly when it was to take place.

He told them about joining the British Army and their relief at him returning from the Spanish Civil War turned into new apprehension. He could of course not tell them about the unusual role he was to undertake but brushed their concerns off by saying he would not be joining a fighting unit.

"So I don't know yet when we can get married, it depends on the army. If I can get a licence we would like it to take place before Christmas."

Terry knew from his intermittent radio contacts with Rich that he was doing teacher training at Chesham Bois School. He met up with him in the Boot and Slipper pub and they were soon deep into reminiscing. Terry told all he could about his experiences in Spain. Rich had been disillusioned by the Munich Agreement between Chamberlain and Hitler and was wavering in his pacifism. He said that he was envious of Terry but it was clear that he really was fully committed to a teaching career. He was nevertheless very honoured to be asked to be Best Man at the wedding.

In view of Terry's army posting a special licence was granted for the wedding which took place five days before Christmas at Chesham registry office. I was a bitter cold, blustery day with easterly winds and a temperature ten degrees below freezing. Terry had rented a flat in the centre of Chesham and they spent their honeymoon buying furniture and curtains and setting up home for the ten days or so before Terry had to report for duty.

As Ashridge was just a short distance from Chesham, he bought a motor-cycle as he thought that he could commute from home. However he was firmly told that it was an entirely residential six-week course and he could have no contact with home whatsoever.

The farewell party was on New Year's Eve. A large party had come over from Ireland for the wedding and were staying in local pubs. The celebration was to prove memorable, with all his family present, as well as Rich with his current girl-friend Doris. They all had difficulty keeping up with the heavy drinking of the Irish. Terry joined in with the dancing and performed a lightning-fast jig that he had learnt many years earlier. He needed all of New Year's Day to recover and the following morning he bade Vivien a tearful farewell and set off through deep snow.

The route to Ashridge was very hilly and the motor-cycle skidded and slid most of the way there with Terry dismounting frequently to push it up the hills. Eventually he arrived at the impressive entrance gates, dismounted and approached the gatehouse.

The Ashridge Estate had been taken over from the original Edgerton family many years previously by the National Trust but the house and garden was sold separately and used as a College of Citizenship for Political Training and Education. However this also acted as perfect cover for a training centre for the Intelligence Service, and it was to this that Terry had been sent.

When he checked in at the gatehouse he was directed by a stoney-faced civilian to the side entrance of the west wing of the house. In contrast he was met by a very affable administrator, Major Stewart, who invited him in and showed him to his room. His accommodation was very comfortable, a large room with a high ceiling and casement windows that looked out over the park. There was a sizeable en-suite bathroom just a little larger than the whole ground floor of his flat in Chesham. Clam thought that this must have been one of the bedrooms of the original family owners.

His first three days consisted of basic drill training, which he had to re-learn as it was different from the training given in the Polish battalion. He grasped it very quickly and went on for a two-day weapons training course. This was very familiar to him but he was introduced to several new weapons that he had not come across before. He realized that some of these had been specially developed for covert operations and could be easily concealed around the body or hidden in small spaces.

The second week consisted of training in unarmed combat. His instructors were two former Shanghai policemen, Bill Fairbairn and Eric Sykes, who had learnt a large number of previously unknown offensive and defensive techniques from the Chinese. As they were unaware of Clam's previous combat experience they were surprised when he rebuffed a simulated attack by Bill Fairbairn and turned it back on him. Fairbairn ended up in a hold that had him within an inch of a broken spine.

After two days of at times vicious sparring with different types of combat, Eric Sykes told Clam that he was as good, if not better than his instructors. Sykes asked him if he would like to become an instructor instead of an agent. He was told that it was intended to set up a special unarmed combat school on a remote estate in Scotland. It sounded attractive at first, but he declined. Spain had given him enough real experience to last him a lifetime. As an agent in the field, he might have to use combat as a last resort, but he did not relish teaching it day after day.

Terry spent the rest of the second and third weeks on wireless telephony training. He soon realized that the technology had moved ahead since his days working in his father's post office, and that the equipment he had used in Spain was very outdated. His amateur radio technique was totally unsuitable for military purposes and so he had to relearn much of what had by now become instinctive.

He had to relearn how to code messages for covert operations, and how to send them in short bursts so that his transmitter could not be detected. He was also introduced to the new compact wireless-transmitter units that were being sent to agents in the field.

During one evening session in which he had been left alone to practice decoding messages, he had quietly contacted Rich, and inquired after Vivien. Rich had told him that she was well, but missing him.

The next morning Terry was summoned to see a very angry Major Stewart. As he stood to rigid attention he was torn off a strip for a breach of security. He was told that all radio transmissions were monitored and that his contact with Rich had been intercepted. Whilst no secret information had been disclosed on this occasion, another transgression would result in a Court Martial.

The next assignment involved a move to Beaulieu House in the New Forest, where Lord Montagu had permitted the intelligence service to establish another training centre. Terry could not inform Vivien of this move, but that was irrelevant anyway as he had been ordered to have no outside contact at all for the duration of his training and he dared not breach security again.

He underwent an intensive course on covert operations and the security procedures necessary to ensure the safety of the intelligence networks. He learnt about the setting up of cells and circuits of agents which had no cross-contact at all, except for one individual. He or she in turn would have only very limited contact with the next layer up in the network. In this way no one security breakdown could affect the rest of the network.

The tradecraft of spying was also taught, including the use of secret codes and inks, and of concealed drop-boxes for messages. The use of explosives was demonstrated as well as the arts of demolition. Terry took to all of this like a duck to water, as much of what he was learning was similar to his activities in Spain.

The whole of this section of training took three weeks and at the end of it Terry was exhausted. It had been lonely work as the training was given one-to-one. Although there were other agents on the course, they were not allowed to meet for security reasons. In this way, if they ever met in the field, they could not compromise each other. His only companion in the little spare time that he had, was Major Stewart, but he had to share his time between all the agents, of which Terry estimated there must have been about six.

Major Stewart was not considered a security risk to the agents as he had been seriously injured in the Great War and would never see service in the field again.

Terry was granted three days leave and was again strongly admonished to say nothing of his assignment. Vivien was overjoyed to see him and they spent most of their time in their little flat, apart from an evening drink with Rich who had just become engaged to Doris. Even then the conversation was a little stilted as Terry was ribbed by his friend for being so reticent about has service life.

Chapter 7
Hullavington

On a cold Tuesday morning in mid February Terry headed off on his motorcycle to Hullavington airfield in Wiltshire. The airfield was less than a year old and destined shortly to be the base for a flying training school, but for the moment it was being used for parachute training of agents and service personnel. It was also used for training of night flights to remote fields for covert deliveries and pick-ups.

Accommodation in the on-site barracks was much more spartan than at Ashridge, with communal dormitories and ablutions. Terry shared his hut with service personnel as all the agents were distributed around the huts for security reasons and were not known to each other. He used his army service real name of Terry Sexton when mixing with the service people, and did his parachute training with them. He assumed that any other agents were similarly training with service personnel from their own huts and so were indistingishable.

Most of the twelve people in Terry's hut were trainee RAF aircrew, doing a three-day course on basic parachuting, that is, sufficient to exit an aircraft in an emergency. Terry joined them for these first three days. The first half of day one was classroom briefing on the basics of using a parachute. The afternoon was given over to practicing landing and everyone had to jump from boxes, land on their feet and then roll over onto the ground. The roll was essential to cushion the impact and Terry learnt how to roll and slap his forearm onto the ground to absorb the energy and break his fall.

Starting from six inches, the jumps were made from progressively higher boxes until, without really realizing it, he was jumping from a twelve-foot high balcony with ease. It was not the case for all of the trainees. One young RAF navigator fell badly and broke his ankle. After he had been taken off to the base hospital, the instructor addressed the remaining trainees, who were all apprehensive after the accident.

"Well, now you know how not to do it! Can anyone tell me what he did wrong?" One tentative hand went up from a Sergeant Pilot.

"Yes sergeant?"

He didn't keep his feet together?" It was more a question than an answer.

"Spot on! I've told you it is essential to keep your ankles together and bend your knees slightly. If your feet are apart, one will hit first and twist you around, then when the other hits it will be twisted and sprain or break. Now you all know, get up there again and do it properly!"

And they did.

The second morning was spent jumping from a high gantry with an actual parachute harness attached to a crane via a drum brake. By varying the brake, jumps could be made at progressively increasing speed. The side of the gantry was a crude representation of the open door of an aircraft. By lunchtime all of the trainees were able to jump with confidence at a realistic landing speed.

After lunch the trainees took turns in groups of six to do actual jumps from the side of a rickety, rattling Whitley bomber specially converted for parachute training. The first jumps were done using a static line linking the parachute pull-cord to the airframe, so the chute deployed automatically as the trainee fell. The second and third jumps were done free fall without the static line and the trainees had to pull the deployment ring on the parachute harness themselves.

All the jumps were successful, with only one sprained ankle and after they had all dined, the servicemen repaired to a pub in nearby Chippenham to celebrate.

The third day consisted of training in jumping from a floor hatch in the aircraft, which was more representative of an actual emergency escape routine. Most heavy aircraft had a hatch in the floor for such emergencies, but the process was not easy. Usually the hatch was covered by other equipment in the aircraft and this had to be removed, not an easy task in a doomed aircraft falling at a steep angle. Secondly the hatch had to be released and either thrown out, or put to one side, depending on the aircraft design. Finally the crew had to escape and this was no easy task. For structural reasons the hatches were not very large, and an airman complete with flying suit and parachute was a very bulky shape.

As aircraft had been developed to fly higher, flying suits had become thicker to keep the wearer warm. In addition, all of the pockets were filled with escape items, maps, basic provisions and weapons. In older aircraft with smaller hatches this made for a very difficult exit.

Each trainee had to make three such jumps and fortunately, by late afternoon, all had passed off without incident. After a short break so that the parachutists could change into their dress uniforms there was a passing-out parade in front of the Station Commander where they were congratulated and handed their parachutist badges to go on their uniforms. Most of them then dispersed back to their home bases, but a few others, clearly trainee agents including Terry, were left and taken away, each into separate quarters.

The day's work was not over for Terry as he then had night jumps to do. Darkness fell quite early as it was in the winter months and he went aloft once more, this time to practice night jumps from the Whitley. He did static line and freefall drops from both the door and hatch of the aircraft, aiming for flares which were lit in the middle of the airfield.

The following morning consisted of one-to-one classwork again, this time on the practice of laying out flare paths for aircraft landing at night and the procedures for quickly disembarking passengers and stores and then reloading. The codes to be used to identify a friendly aircraft and to indicate whether or not it was safe to land were also part of the training.

In the afternoon he was introduced as 'Clam' to another agent, 'Samphire', and they were taken to a remote corner of the airfield. There was already a group of RAF ground crew standing around. They waited for a few minutes until the throaty roar of a radial engine approaching low over the fields was heard. Soon an ungainly high-wing aircraft came in to view. Just as it looked as though it would pass overhead it seemed to almost stop in mid air. There was a mighty crack as the wings seemed to double in size, then the aircraft made an almost vertical descent and landed in front of them. It rolled forwards for just a few yards then stopped and cut its engine.

They knew from the morning's briefing that this was an aircraft called a Lysander, specially designed for aerial reconnaissance. The original aircraft had a single seat in the front cockpit for the pilot, and an observer's seat in the back cockpit, complete with a machine gun for defence. It was equipped with huge flaps and leading-edge slats that opened automatically at low speed to give an excellent short take-off and landing capability.

The aircraft in front of them however, was the prototype of a variant that had been specially modified for covert work. The gun had been removed and two small bench seats fitted in the rear cockpit, one wider than the other. The intention was to be able to carry up to three agents in the rear and to be able to land in small fields in enemy territory. A small ladder had been fitted snugly to the port side beneath the rear cockpit to enable speedy access and a large torpedo-shaped spare fuel tank fitted between the ungainly spatted wheels.

The afternoon's work consisted of practising what had been taught in the morning. With Samphire on one of the passenger benches the Lysander took off and made a circuit to the south-west where there were no inhabitants. Speed was of the essence. As the Lysander returned, the instructor gave a signal and the ground crew ran onto the corner of the airfield and laid out three unlit beacons in an 'L' shape, with the long arm facing into wind. When the aircraft was overhead Terry flashed a bright torch at the Lysander giving the Morse code letter 'R'. The pilot flashed back the correct signal 'S' and flew away a short distance. Terry then gave the instruction to light the three beacons. The Lysander returned and made a short landing along the longest side of the 'L' shape. It immediately turned around and taxied back to the other end of the landing area, and turned into wind once more, ready for a quick getaway.

Both cockpit hoods were slid back and Samphire emerged from the rear one and scuttled down the ladder. At the same time the pilot climbed out of his cockpit and opened a hatch in the side of the aircraft. He removed some boxes and gave them to one of the ground crew. Another member of the ground crew handed him some more boxes and he stowed them away then climbed back into his cockpit. Meanwhile Terry and two more members of the ground crew had quickly climbed into the rear cockpit.

On the ground Samphire flashed the letter 'A' to the pilot who immediately opened up the throttle. The Lysander leapt forward and in just a few yards was airborne and disappearing over the hedges. Inside the rear cockpit Terry and the two airmen were cramped together and barely able to move. After a short circuit the aircraft landed again and they were able to get out.

"Bejasus!" said Terry, stretching his arms and legs as the two airmen did likewise, "I wouldn't want to do that again, never mind about flying hundreds of miles into badlands!"

Samphire shrugged his shoulders and said "We may just have to. Fortunately it won't be often that it'll have to be three of us."

Little did he know.

There were two more practice runs, with variations of duty for the different team members, and then the ground crew were taken back to their barracks. Terry and Samphire then had to practice parachuting from the Lysander. Whilst it was never the intention to carry out an agent insertion by parachuting from the Lysander, in an aircraft emergency, it could be necessary to get out in this way.

There was a complication. For one or two agents in the rear cockpit, wearing parachutes was acceptable but with three passengers the space was so cramped that parachutes could not be worn by the two passengers on the wider bench seat and so they were stowed underneath the bench. In the event of a bale-out they had to retrieve the chutes and put them on but there would be precious little time in which to do it. They had to accept that this was a risk that had to be taken.

The technique for leaving the Lysander by parachute was not difficult but it had to be followed. After jettisoning the canopy the passengers had to undo their seat belts and the one in the rear single seat had then to climb out and down the ladder. It was essential to go all the way to the bottom rung before letting go, otherwise there was a risk of being decapitated by the tailplane. Once the first passenger had left, the second one put on his chute and repeated the exercise, with the third passenger following suit provided there was enough time.

Terry and Samphire climbed aboard the aircraft and it took off yet again. Whilst covert penetration flights could take place at any altitude, near the target area the Lysander had to fly low. This was also the risky time as any damage to the aircraft could result in the need to bale out at anywhere down to three hundred feet. For this exercise however the flight took place at one thousand feet and both passengers made reasonably good landings.

The day was not over however. After dinner the two agents repeated the daytime exercise of landing, changeover and take-off, but this time in the dark with only the torches and beacons to guide them. After two satisfactory exercises they were able to have a few beers, or, in Terry's case, large glasses of Veterano, and go to bed in a now almost empty dormitory.

Chapter 8
Poland

Saturday morning saw Terry biking in to Baker Street where Freddie Younge was waiting to meet him.

"Hello Clam, how was your week? Were you happy with the way it went?"

"Yes it was ok but I was dog tired at the end of it. Very intensive."

"Well that's the way we like to do it, sorts the men from the boys. You'll be pleased to hear that all your instructors passed you with flying colours. Want to see the reports?"

"Not really," said Terry, "I've had enough classwork for one week."

"We feel that its time to put you to work. Things are boiling up, especially in Poland where they think Germany is planning invasion and we think they may be right. Pity is Chamberlain and his appeasers won't act. We have to be prepared and make sure we have a network in place if Poland gets overrun. Do you still have any contacts over there?"

"None that I've been in touch with for years. I could try and contact them but I'm not sure if any phones or post are secure these days."

Terry scratched at his already thinning hair. "That's what we thought. We think that you should go there and try and make direct contact. We need a couple of weeks to brief you but after that you should go. No need for any covert insertion or anything like that. You can go by ferry from Sweden, we will create a cover for you. Any idea where to start?"

"Most of my contacts were around Warsaw. I still have their addresses but of course after all this time they could have moved, but that's the place to start."

"Ok," said Freddie, "Take the rest of the week off and report here on Monday."

"Thanks for your generosity, seeing it's Saturday lunchtime already. I'll be here."

Not quite two days at home were enough to refresh Terry but Vivien made sure that he did not get much sleep.

Over the next two weeks Terry underwent extensive briefing, was given a Polish identity, Milok Toporek, and a full background history of his mythical past and family. He had a refresher course in the Polish language and found that it came back to him almost immediately. He was also given a crash course in refrigeration engineering. This was chosen as his cover in Sweden as his electrical telegraph experience meant that he could pick up the knowledge very quickly.

He was intensively interrogated to see if he could keep his story credible under duress. He was questioned in Polish and German and once or twice he fell for the old trick of suddenly being asked a question in English, but he was soon able to overcome this trait.

The day before he was due to finish the training he was sent to a dentist in St John's Wood. It was evident to Terry that the practice was a cover for a more sinister activity. The dentist examined his mouth and said "I think we have an easy task here. You've already got a large filling in one of your molars so we can have that out. I'll have to enlarge the cavity but it won't take long. Do you want gas?" Terry declined. He had a need to be in control of himself at all times and so had never had anaesthetic for any of his fillings and didn't see the need to start now.

The dentist skilfully re-shaped the cavity and lined it with a gel which quickly hardened. He explained that the cavity was shaped to be slightly concave so that it would retain a cyanide ampoule without the risk of it falling out. The lining gave it some resilience against shock and the ampoule would also be coated in rubber to prevent accidental breakage. He showed Terry a dummy pill and demonstrated how to fit it. He reassured him that if it was accidently swallowed it would pass through unharmed.

"If you need to use it, you have to bite hard on the covering to break the glass. I've got two loaded capsules here for you in this cuff-link box. Fit one at the beginning of a mission, and take it out again afterwards, and be bloody careful!"

"I'm damned if I'll use one!" said Terry, "but I'll take them in case the opportunity arises to force one down the throat of an interrogator!"

When Freddie was satisfied that Terry could stay in character, he was given travel papers and tickets. Terry was given one day's leave to visit his family before setting off for Sweden. When he got home Vivien rushed to greet him and in a flurry of tears of happiness told him that she had just been told by her doctor that she was pregnant, He was over the moon, and that day was one of the happiest of their lives.

In the middle of March he went by ferry to Sweden and the journey was uneventful. He was acutely aware that there were probably foreign agents on the ship but if so, they had been as well trained as he had, for he did not suspect anyone.

As he boarded the ferry he bought a copy of the Daily Express whose headlines told him that Czechoslovakian President Emil Hácha was scheduled to fly to Berlin the next day for a meeting with Adolf Hitler. Speculation was rife that he would be given an ultimatum to allow Germany to occupy his country. The path to war was shortening.

The Swedish immigration officials in Malmo were very thorough. Sweden had declared its neutrality and they knew that agents used the port to try to make entry to other European countries. Sweden was at risk of being declared non-neutral if it could be shown that it was allowing free passage of agents. Terry, or John Rollings as was shown on his passport, was given a thorough grilling.

Why was he travelling to Poland by such a roundabout route? Why had he not just taken a train from France direct across Germany to Warsaw? Why was he staying in Sweden for two days? What was his business?

Fortunately Freddie had prepared him well. The cover for British agents in Sweden was an Import/Export company in Kristianstad and Terry said he was here to negotiate a lucrative contract before going on to do the same in Poland. Yes, he had the contract documents. Yes he had accommodation booked. He was a refrigeration engineer and was contracted to explain the detailed workings of the new range of products. Yes, he had drawings. Would they like to see them? Could he interest them in a refrigerator?

He was kept in a small room for about two hours. Then the officials returned with his documents and with a reluctant technician in tow. They had checked out his meeting in Kristianstad and his accommodation and all was in order, but would he mind if this young engineer asked him a few questions about the refrigerators? He was very interested in them.

It soon became very clear to Terry that the young man knew very little about refrigerators and it transpired that he was a heating technician who had been found doing repair work in the immigration building. Terry was easily able to describe the workings of the refrigerator shown in the drawings and the young man was suitably impressed. Within a short time Terry was released and sent on his way.

He had to take a later train to Kristianstad than planned, and reported in to the Import/Export company offices. The Head of Station was getting concerned when he had not been on the earlier train, but realised why when the immigration office had rang to query Rollings' credentials. On the train Terry had become aware that he was being watched, so during his two-day stay in Kristianstad he went through the motions of visiting the offices for long meetings. He was hosted to a business dinner on the first evening and great play was made with loud friendly chatter about refrigerators. Anyone listening would have been convinced that Rollings was genuine.

A small ferry ran from Kristianstad to Danzig so on the third morning Terry boarded it and settled down for a pleasant trip. It was bitterly cold on deck but he wrapped up well and stayed out to enjoy the crystal-clear skies and deep green sea. He also used it to check for watchers and sure enough, one particular individual seemed to find it necessary to make a lot of excursions out on deck in the area where Terry was sitting. The individual was well muffled up but Terry was able to make out some of his features and his stature and gait. He was sure that he would recognise him again if he saw him.

On arriving in Danzig his reception was very different to that in Sweden. For public consumption he was questioned closely by the immigration officer and then taken to an interview room. Here he was greeted warmly by an intelligence officer who was expecting him. The Poles had been briefed about his mission by the British Ambassador and were grateful that the British were supporting them at a time of great danger. Any help that could be given would be well received. By previous arrangement they provided him with his Polish Government identity documents as Milok Toporek, which he had not risked carrying via Sweden. In these he was described as a health worker who was convalescing and recently discharged from hospital having contracted tuberculosis at work.

After being briefed by the intelligence officer Terry was released from the interview room and made his way to the exit of the building where he hailed a taxi. As he climbed in he noticed the muffled man from the ship get into another taxi, only this time he was not muffled up and Terry got a good look at his face. He had been briefed that both taxis would actually be from the Polish intelligence service and as his own taxi exited the dockyard and turned left, a large lorry pulled across in front of the second one, barring its exit. The taxi driver made feeble attempts to get around it but when the lorry eventually pulled very slowly away, Terry's taxi was long gone, taking some back streets to double back and set off in a different direction.

The taxi was in fact a very comfortable car with a powerful heater to counter the bitter cold outside. The car took Terry all the way to Warsaw, a drive of about seven hours. He and the driver both kept a lookout for any following cars but none could be detected.

The driver stopped once for a comfort break and to eat a sandwich but neither spoke a word to each other for the whole trip. For Terry there were thermos flasks of coffee and potato soup in the car, and a bottle of Polish vodka with a box of caviar. He gestured to the driver through the rear view mirror, holding up the vodka bottle, but the driver waved back, raised his own bottle and grinned. Terry would have preferred to have his Veterano, but if he had brought some with him it would have been a complete gave-away to the Swedish customs.

When they arrived in Warsaw the driver took him to his hotel, a small discreet house in the Jewish quarter. Terry had had a very long day and went straight to bed intent on an early start the following morning.

Over breakfast he made polite conversation with the hotel owner and found that his Polish language was accepted without query. He then went back to his room to gather some papers and set out to try and contact his old friends and to start to set up a network of circuits for British Intelligence.

Chapter 9
Warsaw

Terry found Warsaw was very different from his earlier visits. Everywhere there were military vehicles and most men were dressed in military uniforms of one service or another. Road checks and spot checks at hotels took place randomly, but his Toporek Polish identity documents were accepted without question because they were, after all, genuine.

The tight security made him very cautious so instead of trying to get in touch with his old contacts immediately, he set about reconnoitring their old haunts in the suburbs of the city. In the bistros where he had eaten with the Marxist Academics group in 1936 he searched in vain for any of the students or lecturers with whom he had exchanged ideas and caroused.

He had spent only a few days in Warsaw on that earlier visit but had become friendly with two of the lecturers at the University and a journalist, Isaac Deutscher, and had visited all three at their homes. All three were members of the Bolshevik-Leninist movement, of which the academic group were an offshoot, but Terry had lost touch with them when he renounced his communist affiliation. Nevertheless he decided to see if they were still in residence.

Sitting in the tiny hotel lounge he started by scanning the newspapers kindly provided by the proprietor. These were however just a few of the more popular dailies. Deutscher had been a freelance journalist who wrote mainly for the more serious newspapers and the left-wing press and Terry found no columns written by his old friend in these papers. It became clear in fact that the newspapers were all heavily censored and full of anti-Fascist, anti-Communist propaganda and anti-Semitic sentiments, so he wrapped himself up well and set off to find a newsagent.

He found one in the same block as his hotel and went inside to scan the shelves. He recognised only two of the newspapers that he remembered from his earlier visits but their content was entirely changed. The leader columns were sheer propaganda and he could find no serious comment or articles by independent journalists. Searching the magazine shelves he could not find any of these that he recognised. None of the newspapers or magazines that he scanned had any articles by Deutscher. He decided that the only way he would be able to track him down would be to start at his home.

Deutscher had lived in a Jewish residential zone but when Terry arrived in the area he could see straight away that it had been vandalised and that many of the properties were empty. Apart from some military patrols there were no people about and he felt very conspicuous as he made his way to Dluga Street where he had visited Deutscher and his wife. Many of the properties had broken windows and antisemitic slogans were painted on the walls and gates to the houses.

Terry strolled slowly along the pavement on the opposite side of the road past Deutscher's house and could see right away that it had been abandoned. The house next door seemed to be still inhabited with neat curtains at the window and a front door devoid of graffiti, unlike many of the other houses in the street. Terry continued his stroll to the far end of the street whilst debating with himself whether or not to go back to the house. Eventually he spun on his heel and headed purposefully back to the house of Deutscher's neighbour. It was a long time before anyone answered his knock, but the door did not open. A querulous woman's voice from behind the door asked him who he was.

"My name is Milok Toporek, I'm an old friend of Isaac Deutscher, and I wondered if you knew where I can find him?"

" No I don't. They've gone away." She replied sharply.

"I can see that, but did they leave a forwarding address?"

"No, they've gone away. I don't know where they are. Please leave me alone."

Realising that this approach was getting him nowhere, Terry set off to return to his hotel room to think out what to do next, but at the end of the street he was stopped by two soldiers who examined his papers and questioned him closely about what he was doing in the street. As his papers appeared to be in order he was allowed to proceed but he realised that he would have to be very careful about where he went.

Back in his room he thought that there was a good chance that his two lecturer friends at the University of Warsaw would still be in post. But what if they weren't? From his reading of the newspapers he knew that the Polish government was profoundly suspicious of any communist activity and was suppressing and censoring anything related to it. He was also concerned that German and communist agitators were stirring up anti-Semitism. The two lecturers' subjects were politics and economics, with a strong Marxist leaning. Terry doubted if they would still have jobs. Nevertheless, with no other option he set off towards the university campus area.

Despite the extensive devastation he was able to recognise the various buildings of the different faculties and he went into the entrance of the Economics Faculty. Instead of the pretty young receptionist that he remembered from his pre-war days the front office was occupied by an overweight soldier who must have been at least sixty years old, and who looked at Terry suspiciously and demanded to know what he wanted.

"I'm thinking of applying for a post-graduate course in the department, and wondered if you had some information on what is available." It became immediately obvious that the guard had little interest and even less knowledge about academic matters because he asked to see Terry's identity papers and interrogated him about why he wanted to study economics. Terry had a story ready prepared and told the guard that he was an invalid and could not do heavy work but wanted to educate himself until he was fit again. This tied in with the hospital discharge papers in his documents and so the guard grudgingly gave him some syllabus papers about available courses and post-graduate vacancies.

Terry thanked him and went out of the building to find somewhere to read the faculty documents. Near the entrance gate he found a bench already occupied at one end by a man who from his dress was clearly a student. Leafing through the papers swiftly he soon saw that neither of his old contacts was listed among the staff of the department, nor did he recognise any of the names. Seeing what he was reading, the student struck up a conversation. "Looking to start a course?" he asked. "I wouldn't bother. All the lecturers are political appointments here to push the government agenda."

"Why would they do that?" queried Terry, although he knew the answer.

"Because many of the previous lecturers were Marxists, and the government hates communists almost as much as it hates fascists." Terry deduced from the bitter tone of the student that he was probably a communist sympathiser, and cagily led him on. "I was acquainted with one or two of the lecturers, but they don't appear in the schedule of staff in this syllabus."

"Well I have only been studying here a year so I don't know any of the earlier lecturers, but I think that some are still teaching privately. What were their names?"

"If I remember right, there was a Ginsburg, Szymon Ginsburg, and a Lucjan Klimowicz. Szymon lectured in politics and Lucjan in Economics."

A flash of apprehension shot across the student's face for a second, then he asked suspiciously "Who are you, where are you from?"

"Milok Toporek," and he thrust out his hand affably. "From Warsaw, but I've been working abroad for over two years." His worry that the student might have been an informer sent to follow him, evaporated when he realised that the student was as apprehensive as he had been. "The truth is, I have a lot in common with these friends of mine and want to see if they are alright."

The student took his outstretched hand diffidently and said "Janos Rumkowski, student of economics. What was your connection with them?"

Sensing that he could be more open, Terry said "We used to meet at communist Internationale meetings here in Warsaw and in Moscow before the Spanish civil war started, then I went off to fight." I have just got back and wanted to look them up. It looks as though I am out of luck."

"Not entirely," said Rumkowski, brightening pertceptibly, "I can help you, at least part way. Szymon was discharged from his post and suffered badly from anti-Semitic attacks. I don't know where he went. But Lucjan Klimowicz is still here, but he was also discharged and is not supposed to work. The only way he can earn a living is by teaching secretly. Now in fact, he teaches me privately, so I can learn the truth, instead of all this propaganda! I think he has several students like me, but he keeps very quiet about it."

"Can you tell me where he lives?" Terry asked. Rumkowski stood up and said "Better than that, I can take you there."

Klimowicz lived close to the university campus in a single bedroom apartment with his wife and young son. His happiness at seeing Toporek, or Terry Sexton as he knew him was swiftly replaced by concern. "Come inside, quickly! You too Janos!" Klimowicz swiftly ushered them into the tiny living room and Rumkowski looked bemused when Terry was introduced to his wife. Terry had to quickly explain about his Toporek alias.

Lucjan Klimowicz said anxiously "But you shouldn't be here Terry, it's far too dangerous! The police and military are on the look-out for strangers in Warsaw, seeking out

German or Russian agents. Everyone knows war is coming and the authorities are paranoid." Terry asked if he could speak privately to him and they went into the bedroom and shut the door. Terry had to explain that he no longer supported the communists but was working for the British and Polish governments to establish a resistance network in anticipation of the war. He asked Lucjan where his sympathies lay.

"I am still a communist of course, but I am Polish first. If called up, I shall fight the Germans. If not, I and some friends are already planning to resist. Janos is one of them and I have some other students who are also preparing to join us."

Over the next few months Terry was able to establish a number of circuits of agents, initially in the Warsaw area, but gradually extending over most of Poland using Klimowicz' connections. By an understanding between London and Warsaw the Polish government deliberately avoided interfering so as not to compromise the network if Poland should be over-run and the government forced to flee. This proved to be a very prescient move.

Chapter 10
War

Cedric Attenby was furious. On the morning of 31st March 1939 the Prime Minister had announced an Anglo-Polish Agreement which gave a guarantee to the Polish nation of support in the event of any threat to Polish independence. This followed the German occupation of Czechoslovakia in defiance of the Munich Agreement. However, straight after the announcement the British foreign Minister Lord Halifax had told the press that he did not think that the Polish agreement was a binding one. This was widely reported on the news networks and caused uproar in Poland as well as Baker Street.

Cedric had already had a cyphered message from Terry to say that his newly-recruited agents were agitating to know what was going on. He was concerned that his nascent network would fall apart before it got off the ground. Cedric insisted on a meeting with the Minister and forcibly expressed his disgust at the lack of cohesion in the Government. The Minister said he would see what he could do to get reassurance for the Poles.

It wasn't until a week later when the Polish Foreign Minister made a hasty visit to London that an agreement to a formal Anglo-Polish Military Alliance was reached.

It was agreed that a much-respected British officer and diplomat Major-General Sir Colin McVean Gubbins would lead a delegation to Poland to thrash out the details.

The delegation left for Warsaw in the middle of April to conduct negotiations. However Gubbins' dual task was also to plan a joint programme of sabotage and guerrilla fighting in the event of an invasion by Germany. With the announcement of the Military Alliance, Terry's agents had been mollified and as the head of this new espionage network he was ordered to join the talks, ostensibly as an interpreter. He struck up an immediate friendship with Gubbins who was not generally known for his affability.

With good progress being made, the delegation returned to England and Terry remained in Poland continuing to work building up his intelligence circuits whilst at the same time working with the Polish General Staff on sabotage plans.

Gubbins returned with his delegation in July with plans for shipments of arms and financial support. Terry was again involved in the plans but just after Gubbins had left, the Polish intelligence service announced a big development. They claimed to have made a breakthrough in cracking the Enigma code and invited British code breakers to visit.

A delegation of code breakers from BP and from the French cipher school was hastily arranged and they arrived in Warsaw in mid July and met with the three Polish code breakers who had made the discovery. Terry arranged the meeting to take place in one of his covert locations in the Kabackie Woods on the outskirts of Warsaw and he acted as one of the interpreters.

The lead cipher expert from BP was Dillwyn Knox, an expert whose successes dated back to the Great War. His code breaking skills had been a direct influence on the entry of the United States into the war. To Terry's disgust, he learnt that Knox had cracked Franco's Enigma code using the machine rescued by him, but had not told the Republicans because he favoured Franco's Nationalists. Knox was highly strung and totally frustrated at his inability to crack the German Enigma.

The three Polish cipher analysts then revealed their methods. They showed the delegations some Wehrmacht Enigma machines and demonstrated their techniques. They used a combination of perforated paper sheets and devices called Cyclometers and Bombas. These consisted of primitive Enigma machines connected back to back and mechanised so as to be able to analyse a wide range of setting combinations in a short space of time. They then announced to general amazement that they had been breaking German Enigma codes since 1932.

The reason for their success was that the three Polish code breakers were mathematicians. Up until this point, code-breaking had been considered a linguistic skill, and classical scholars had been recruited as cipher breakers with a great deal of success. The Poles recognised however that the Enigma machine performed mathematical transformations and so recruited mathematics experts who used matrix analysis to find solutions.

The British and French delegates were astounded. Knox, who had a classical background and was famed also for deciphering fragments of ancient writings on papyrus, almost had a nervous breakdown on the spot. There were so many questions to be answered, so much to learn. How had the Poles obtained the German Enigmas? They were amazed when they were told that the Poles had made them themselves by calculating mathematically how the rotors were wired internally.

There was a further surprise. The Poles said that a recent addition by the Germans of two new rotors had made the number of combinations of codes beyond the reach of Polish capability. With the prospect of imminent war they realised that they desperately needed outside help. They were therefore handing over all their results to the British and French in the hope that the work could be carried on. Furthermore they were giving three of the Enigma machines to each of the delegations.

After more exchanges of information the discussion turned to how to get the Enigmas back to England. As there were three it was decided to send them by three different routes. The paperwork including the large perforated sheets and one machine would be sent back by diplomatic bag using the normal cross-country channels. A second machine would be carried by a courier and taken via Switzerland and through France.

The third machine would be taken by Terry in a covert Whitley bomber. As a result of the Gubbins delegations a Whitley had been fitted with long range fuel tanks and was to be used to deliver a large quantity of arms, explosives, W/T sets and other equipment to Poland in the first week of August. As far as Terry was concerned there were included two other vital crates. The Thatched Barn Disguise Section had provided a quantity of clothing suited to a range of localities and nationalities for agents in the field. Station Fourteen had provided also a mass of false identity papers, passes, food coupons and other paperwork necessary for travelling across enemy-occupied territory.

Terry was scheduled to return in the aircraft to report back to Baker Street and to help train more agents. He would take the Enigma with him. In the event of an accident he would ensure that an explosive charge would destroy any evidence of the cipher machine.

The Whitley took off from RAF Marham just before dusk on the sixth of August and staggered into the air with its heavy cargo. The type had been designed to take off from grass fields but because of its heavy fuel load and cargo of supplies for Poland, Marham had been chosen because it was one of the new generation of airfields with concrete runways. The aircraft lumbered across the flat countryside of Norfolk, slowly gaining height until it reached the North Sea. Even with its additional fuel tanks and a reduced economy speed of two hundred and ten miles per hour, the Whitley was at the extreme of its range for Warsaw, so it was flying as high as was prudent to minimise fuel consumption.

The pilot was taking a route across the North Sea to Jutland, cutting across Denmark at the shortest point several miles north of Tonder and Sonderborg. As he approached the coast he dived the aircraft to gain speed and cut across the neck of land at below four hundred feet, to minimise the risk of being seen by observers or German agents who were known to be present in the area. Once over the sea again he had to weave his way amongst the islands of Zealand and at last reached the Baltic Sea, as far as he knew, undetected.

The Whitley made its way eastwards keeping at the same low altitude and well away from the north coast of Germany. When it reached Danzig the pilot banked south west and crossed into the Danzig corridor. He knew that this was the most dangerous part of the journey. The corridor had been ceded to Poland after the Great War to give the country access to the sea. It was home to many German-speaking people who were agitating, together with Hitler, for the return of the corridor to Germany. As the area was very hilly the pilot had to climb the aircraft to a safe height and risked thereby being spotted. Any unknown intrusion into the corridor was likely to be taken as a provocation and could stir unrest.

Before long, just as dawn was breaking, the pilot could pick out the Vistula river and he turned to follow its relatively straight course to Warsaw. He located his destination, Mokotów airfield and flashed his identification sign. Landing instructions were flashed by Morse code to him and he was soon on the ground.

Polish Air Force ground crew, Terry, with other members of the underground network were waiting, and swarmed around the aircraft as the cargo was unloaded. Terry took charge of the precious W/T sets that had been sent for his network, as well as the crates of clothing and fake documents. He entrusted some of them to two of his agents and they each set off for different bases. There the sets would be cached prior to distribution to the partisans in each circuit.

As it was now daylight the return trip could not take place until evening so the aircraft was re-fuelled and serviced before being moved to a hanger. Mokotów was a grass airfield but as the aircraft was low on fuel when it landed it was well within limits. Similarly for the take-off, without the heavy cargo, a grass field was adequate.

Terry returned at nine in the evening, driven in a motor-cycle combination by one of his agents. Together with his precious Enigma cargo he had also been given the Cyclometer and more documentation on the Polish code breaking so he was well loaded down as he got out of the sidecar.

The take-off was very bumpy but the old Whitley leapt into the air in a rather more sprightly way than before. With its lighter load it could fly at over two hundred and thirty miles per hour. The return flight was uneventful and Terry was back on the ground at Marham by four in the morning and immediately loaded his valuable packages into the waiting car. By seven in the morning he was in the Baker Street offices.

It was far too early for Cedric Attenby's sensibilities, but Reggie Hawthorne was waiting to meet him.

"Hello Crab old boy!" (Reggie was never very good at code names) "So you made it! Jolly good show. We'll get it up to BP as soon as we can. The other two Enigmas have already arrived safely, and Dilly Knox is busy beavering away trying to crack 'em. Seems to have recovered from the initial shock and now there's no stopping him."

"I'm glad to hear it," said Terry, "what's the latest? All sorts of rumours are buzzing around in Poland, talk of imminent war."

"Just rumours old boy. Despite the agreement, Chamberlain and Halifax will never go to war over Poland. Mind you, Winston is doing all he can to stir it up. Bloody warmonger!"

"Well I can tell you, without a word of a lie, if the balloon goes up and we don't go to help them, the Poles will declare war on us! Feelings are running very high over there."

Reggie shrugged. Well, it's not our problem. Let Whitehall sort it out. We have our job to do and we'll just get on with it. How's your network coming along?"

"Just fine," responded Terry "I've got seven circuits pretty well up and running and another four in embryo. Those W/T sets you've sent will make a world of difference. Now I need to get some more recruits from over here to come out and help. If Germany attacks, I want to be able to extend our network back into the Fatherland and listen in to Adolf on his home ground."

"We've anticipated that. There's a course running up at Ashridge at the moment and you can take your pick, at least after Gubbins has had his. He's sending another delegation out to Poland at the end of the month. What's your timescale?"

"A week. Home for a day, then there's another bloody Wobbly Whitley going back in six days time and I intend to be on it. You really should do something to get a decent aircraft for the trip. The Flying Barn Door is far too slow and hasn't got the altitude. It would be a sitting duck in the event of war."

We're trying as hard as we can but Bomber Command are hanging on to their new heavies like grim death. We were lucky to get a Whitley. It's obsolete but they're still making them because the new heavies aren't ready yet in sufficient numbers."

A week later, his recruiting well under way, Terry with two novice agents boarded the Whitley and repeated the journey to Warsaw. The takeoff was delayed by two hours owing to the need to change a magneto and as a result it was starting to get light as they entered the Danzig corridor. There had been riots in Danzig during the week with German-speaking inhabitants demanding re-unification with Germany, but there was no interference with the flight.

When they landed they were greeted with the news that Germany had just signed a non-aggression pact with Soviet Russia. This was devastating news for the Poles as it could only be a prelude to invasion.

Two days later the invasion of Poland started and on the third of September The United Kingdom and France declared war on Germany. By the middle of the month the German troops had covered half of the territory of Poland. On the seventeenth of September the Soviet Union declared war on Poland and shortly afterwards they met the German army halfway across the country.

As the invaders advanced, Terry's network sprang into action. He had set up eleven networks across Poland and infiltrated partisan agents into several junior positions in the administration. However as the invaders swept across the country they arrested many senior Polish officials and the result was that a few of the more junior staff were promoted. Clam was thus able to get access to more useful information.

One particular agent, Limpet, was in a particularly fortuitous position. His real name was Dietmar Hoffman and he had a German father and a Polish mother. His father had been a salesman for a German machine tools company and had been based in Poland before the war, where he met and married Dietmar's mother Martyna. Thus the boy had dual nationality. Like many middle class professionals the senior Hoffman had joined the Nazi Party in the middle of the 1930s but had taken no active role. The family home was in Cracow and when Dietmar was thirteen years old his father died of heart disease. His mother took the boy back to her family in Lvov and he left school at fifteen to start work as a clerk in local government.

When the Wehrmacht reached Lvov many Poles were arrested and sent back to Germany as slave labour. Because of Dietmar's nationality and the fact that his mother was receiving a Nazi widow's pension, they were allowed to stay. However to Martyna's consternation her parents and sister were sent to Germany. The Wehrmacht were setting up administrative offices in each town and Dietmar was sent to work in the Lvov headquarters. Dietmar and his mother became extremely anti-Nazi because of the way their family had been treated and it was here that the head of the South East network of the resistance recruited him and gave him the name 'Limpet'.

The usually thorough Nazi administration was in some disarray, largely because of the unexpectedly speed with which they had advanced, and because they had to contend with the westward push of the Russian front. As a result Limpet's German name and passport was taken as read and he was promoted to a junior communications post in which he had to pass routine messages over landlines to Wehrmacht dispositions. He had been able to pass some of the more useful information back to his circuit head.

Chapter 11
Sikorski

Major-General Gubbins and his further delegation to Poland arrived in Warsaw by coincidence on the third of September, the day that Britain declared war. Terry once again joined the group as an interpreter and the delegation set to work urgently with the Polish Chiefs of Staff to cement plans for joint working. Terry's partisan networks were already playing havoc behind the German lines using equipment already supplied but these would soon run out. Co-ordination with the Polish Underground movement was essential.

The delegation could not go home by the same route and as the situation in Warsaw became more precarious they, together with the Polish Government Ministers made their escape via Rumania and Paris. Terry went with them, leaving his trusted Second in Command Bruno Wronski, 'Oyster', to run his network.

It was whilst he was on his way to Paris that he contacted Rich on his portable short-wave radio. Rich told him that Vivien had given birth to a baby girl the day before. Terry asked him to send Vivien his love and to say that he hoped to be home soon for a short while. Rich also told him that in view of the ominous situation in Europe, he and Doris were getting married in two weeks time. Would Terry be around to be his Best Man? Terry told him that it might be difficult because he did not know where he might be as the situation was so fluid.

The exile of the Polish Government created a political upheaval and it resigned en masse. General Wladyslaw Sikorski became the new Prime Minister and Commander in Chief on the first of October and immediately began consultations. Sikorski had a highly successful diplomatic and military background but had fallen out with the previous administration and been denied any role either civil or military. He now set about trying to bring unity to the country and set up his new Government in Exile in Paris.

Sikorski appointed some new Chiefs of Staff and called them together with the leaders of the Polish Underground and of the British intelligence network in Poland. Terry was introduced and explained about the network he had set up and the sabotage that it was already carrying out. Sikorski listened carefully to all that was said and decided to travel to London to talk to Gubbins himself to negotiate more weaponry and finance.

A few days later General Sikorski met with Major General Gubbins in London. They had crossed paths many years earlier and greeted each other like old friends. Terry had been brought along by Sikorski to act as translator because, although the General's English was excellent, many of his party could not speak the language.

They soon got down to business and it was agreed that covert activities of sabotage and demolition would be co-ordinated from a group specially set up in London by the British Chiefs of Staff. Sikorski would have the right of appeal in the event of major disagreement. It was also agreed that all covert activity except for some minor sabotage events would be put on hold until resources had been built up to an effective level. Gubbins promised that the United Kingdom would provide the Polish Government in Exile with sufficient funds for weaponry and to carry on its activities in Paris.

That evening Gubbins hosted a dinner for Sikorski's party and also for a number of senior Poles who had fled to England. Sikorski took the opportunity to hand out medals to many of those present. This was something that he was to become in the habit of doing wherever he went.

A private talk with Winston Churchill who was an old friend of Sikorski's took place the following morning, followed by a meeting with the Prime Minister Neville Chamberlain in the afternoon. Terry was of course not present at these meetings but he later left with Sikorski to inspect formations of escapee Polish troops who were forming up in different parts of the country. Sikorski found his presence invaluable, not only as a translator but also because of his deep military experience.

At the end of the three day trip General Sikorski flew back to Paris whilst Terry went to the Baker Street offices to see Cedric Attenby and report on the turbulent events of the last few weeks. He also said that he wanted to get back to Poland as soon as possible. Cedric said that this was virtually impossible as with hostilities raging in the country and German airspace alive with aircraft, the lumbering Whitley would not stand a chance if it was caught on the ground unloading. He told Terry to go home for a few days to see his new family, and to report back in a week.

Back in Chesham Terry walked into a happy family gathering. Vivien had just come out of the maternity hospital and was home in bed with the new baby and her parents and in-laws around her. Rich was there too with Doris. They decided that the baby would be called Sarah, a name that was very popular at the time.

Now with a family Terry and Vivien decided that it was time to buy their own home. He had a backlog of pay in his bank account and it was sufficient to put down on a deposit on a small semi in Amersham. With the help of his parents and his in-laws he was able to furnish the house, with Vivien giving instructions on decor from her bed.

Rich and Doris' wedding was on the Saturday before Terry had to report back so he was able to fulfil his pleasant duty as Best Man. It was just a very small intimate event and Vivien was able to attend with Sarah, having been declared fully recovered from her confinement. The next day, Sunday, was Sarah's christening, so Terry had been able to pack in a great deal on his short visit.

Back in Baker Street on the Monday morning, Terry tried another tack with Cedric. He told him that at Marham he had seen shockproof canisters being loaded with equipment to be parachuted into inaccessible locations. These were designed to be dropped from Wellington bombers in the Far East theatre. His proposal was to arrange for some trials with the old Whitley bomber to see if another provisioning run to Warsaw could be carried out using an aerial drop. He would parachute in at the same time. At last Cedric reluctantly agreed to at least attempt the trials.

The problem with the Whitley was that the floor hatch was too small for the canisters and could not be enlarged for structural reasons. So, reasoned Terry, let's re-arrange the canister mountings to slide out of the side door. All it would require was a wooden ramp to slide the canisters up over the lip of the door. The next requirement was for yet another auxiliary fuel tank if the aircraft was to make the round trip. As it was, it was going to have to land in France to re-fuel on the way back.

With the help of ground crew at Marham he made the necessary modifications and arranged some trial drops over the airfield. These went off very well and it was possible to time the drops to land with good accuracy. The drops were then practiced at night and accuracy actually improved owing to the clear view of the lights around the drop zone.

He now had the difficult task of persuading Cedric Attenby to let him make the journey. There was a growing pile of weaponry, provisions and explosives for Poland in a sealed hanger at Marham but the decision had been made to wait until the New Year when a more powerful Halifax bomber would become available. However by the end of October Poland had been largely pacified and military activity by both the Germans and Russians had settled down. Terry badgered Attenby until he gave in and agreed to the flight.

Terry radioed Oyster and gave him the code words for where the drop was to take place and when. He had chosen a night just three days after the full moon so it would be fairly dark for the crossing of the Baltic, but with a rising moon as they approached the drop zone. Any enemy ships or night fighters would have difficulty spotting them on the long sea transit. The risky time would be following the Vistula down to Warsaw and Kampinoski Park where the agents would be waiting for the pick-up.

The first of November came and Terry rode across to Marham to watch the Whitley being loaded. The canisters were filled with all the goods from the hanger and he estimated they must have weighed over three tons. There were over twenty of the canisters and each was connected to a rail inside the bomber by a static line which would open the parachute. Together with a full load of fuel in the main tanks and auxiliary tanks the aircraft was well over its maximum take-off weight.

As darkness fell Terry and two more novice agents climbed aboard the Whitley and settled down into a cramped space forward of the neatly stacked and secured canisters. The instruction to take off was given and the long thin aircraft lumbered into the air just short of the end of the runway.

All went well until they were about fifty miles short of Danzig. Suddenly tracer bullets flashed past the windscreen as an unseen night fighter attacked from behind. The pilot had little room for manoeuvre at five hundred feet but he immediately put the aircraft into corkscrew turns and dropped the altitude to less than one hundred feet, skimming over the water's surface just a wingspan below. The fighter lost sight of the Whitley in the turns and could not safely descend to look for it so the flight continued on its original course but at a suicidal height.

As they approached Danzig the pilot had to climb to make the inland turn and to clear the hills. At an altitude of just seven hundred feet he crossed the Danzig corridor, now in German hands, and located the Vistula. He followed the river to Warsaw and then, using dead reckoning, turned to locate Kampinoski Park.

Just as the pilot thought he must have missed it, the Morse letter 'W' was flashed up from a black area just beneath him. He quickly replied with a 'Z' and a circle of lights appeared below, dimly outlining a clearing in the park. The pilot switched on a red 'Standby!' light in the fuselage and the three agents leapt up and started to organise the canisters. The side door to the fuselage was opened and the first canister set in the entrance. They waited as the aircraft was lined up for its first run in. When the red light changed to green they pushed canisters out one after another until the red light came on again. They did the same thing for the second and third run by which time all the canisters had gone. They hauled in the trailing static lines from the canisters and stowed them.

Terry squeezed through the cockpit entrance and shouted "All canisters gone! Just we three now!" The pilot gave the thumbs up sign and turned for his final run. As he did so he climbed to one thousand feet to give plenty of time for the chutes to open as the agents were free-falling. The co-pilot would retrieve the static lines and close the fuselage door.

On the final run the red light had just come on when anti-aircraft fire started to come up towards them. On seeing the green light the three agents exited the aircraft. Terry was last and as he fell he saw a direct flak hit on the starboard engine. His chute opened and he floated down, but he saw the Whitley turn away with flames flickering from the stricken engine. It was a Mark 2 aircraft so he knew that it could maintain height on one engine, but wondered if the increased fuel consumption would prevent it getting back to France.

On the ground the three agents collected together their parachutes and met up with Oyster and the partisan group. All the canisters were found and loaded into a lorry and driven to a safe store deep within the woods. By the time any German forces arrived the agents were all long gone and any traces of their presence erased.

Over the next two months Terry set about completing his network of eleven circuits, each one isolated from the others for security reasons. In his daily reports to London he found out that the Whitley had got dangerously low on fuel and landed in Holland, where the crew had destroyed it before being interned for the rest of the war.

Christmas came and went and in the New Year's Honours list Cedric Attenby got his knighthood. At a select party in his office he intimated that the true reason for the honour was the Service's success in bringing home the Enigma secrets and that the real person responsible for the honour was not present, but in Poland.

Early in January 1940 orders came through to Terry that full-scale partisan activities could begin and so their well-laid plans were put into effect. It was particularly stressful for the Poles, for after each sabotage attack SS detachments would carry out reprisal raids.

The heads of each circuit met with Terry to discuss what to do about the situation. At first they selected targets remote from any village in the hope that the SS would not know who to blame but this did not work as reprisals were carried out indiscriminately. They were having a serious effect because the local populations were enraged by the reprisals and blamed the underground networks, and several partisans were betrayed. Despite this the Polish partisans bravely voted to carry on with the sabotage activities and bear the consequences.

In May news came through that Neville Chamberlain had resigned and that Winston Churchill had become Prime Minister. On the same day German troops had invaded the Low Countries and were attacking French and British positions. A day later a coded order came addressed to Clam. Terry was to return to England immediately.

'Immediately' was a relative term in war-torn Poland. To get back to England Terry had to use his false German identity and make the dangerous crossing through Germany to Switzerland. It took him two weeks to reach that neutral country and then he had to make a transit through into France. He did not dare risk trying to pass through immigration so he took a tortuous route through the mountains. During May the Swiss had mobilised their army although it was not deployed. However border guards were reinforced so Terry had to pick his way very carefully between the patrols.

He found that northern France was rapidly being overtaken by German forces so instead he was able skirt round the southern flanks to travel to Angers where Sikorski had moved his Government in Exile from Paris as the situation deteriorated. Terry reported to General Sikorski's office and was warmly received. However France was by now on the point of capitulation and the Polish Government in Exile were preparing to move yet again to England. On the twelfth of June Terry shared their flight to Northolt and reported in to Sir Cedric Attenby the next morning.

Chapter 12
France

"Where the devil have you been for the last month! Don't you know there's a war on?"

Sir Cedric was in an irascible mood.

Terry ignored the question and said as sweetly as he could muster "Congratulations Sir Cedric. I hear you have been given a knighthood. Very well deserved, I must say."

"Never mind that. The whole service is in a mess. We've been caught short and need to get more agents into Europe as quickly as we can. We want you to go to France and get a network set up as soon as possible. We've had freshly trained agents here sitting on their arses for weeks waiting for you to get back."

"What about Poland?" asked Terry. "I've just got that going very nicely, what are they going to do?"

"I'm sure that Oyster will carry on well enough in Warsaw. He has done ok so far in your, I dare to say, very prolonged absence. The Nazis will be in Paris by tomorrow as the French have declared it an open city. Now there's already a Resistance movement out there that was set up as a precaution after Munich. There are over twenty thousand Poles in France, mainly legal residents but also refugees from Germany and from the Spanish Civil War. You probably know many of them so you'll need to establish contact. We'll drop you there, probably near Blois and have a reception party waiting to take you into hiding. You can take two new agents with you. The modified Lysander's got three passenger seats so we might as well make use of them."

"I know all about bloody Lysander seats, they're as cramped as hell. I'll make sure to get two skinny agents and hope I can still feel my legs when we arrive," said Terry . "Can I have a day to see my family?"

"Yes of course. It'll take that long to organise the flight. You'll be flying from Tangmere on the south coast. It's the nearest for the crossing to the Loire and we're planning to set up a complete squadron of Lysanders there next year when we get this variant into full production. Westland have their hands full at the moment because in France the air observation Lysanders are sitting ducks. We've had more than a hundred shot down over the last six weeks and they can't keep up with replacements.

I suggest you go off this afternoon to pick your agents and then go home. It could be a long stint in France."

Terry was glad to do as he was told. He read the training reports of the new agents to try and select the best. However his final decision was based on their weight and height. He wanted as comfortable a trip as possible in the Lysander. He interviewed the two selected candidates, a twenty-five year old man and a twenty-three year old woman. Both had passed out close to the top of the training schedules so he was satisfied that, with some intense on-the-spot experience that they would both prove to be excellent circuit leaders.

Terry decided that for the French network the agents' code names should be those of birds. Michael Fletcher was an incredibly tall, thin and handsome young man with a lock of hair that persistently flopped over his face. He wore his clothes loosely but in such a casual style as to appear roguish. Terry named him 'Jay'.

Marianne Escot was the opposite. Petite and barely five feet tall she was of mixed French and English parentage. She had been brought up mostly in Alsace but her parents had moved to England in 1936 soon after Germany had re-occupied the Saar. She was fiercely patriotic and brilliantly intelligent, a strategic thinker. Terry name her 'Wren'. He spent the rest of the afternoon briefing the two about the forthcoming flight to France. He then left for home in Amersham to have the next two days with Vivien and Sarah, who had grown incredibly in the months whilst he was away. She was alert and curious and crawling all round the flat, occasionally pulling herself up against a piece of furniture. It would not be long before she was walking, and Terry had missed so much.

On the evening of the second day Terry received a single word telephone call, 'Spider'. He knew that the flight was on for the following night. He spent the following morning visiting his parents and Rich and Doris, then called in to Baker Street to receive a final briefing from Sir Cedric with Jay and Wren. His alias was to be Patrice Lefebre, a French farm labourer. The three of them went by car to Tangmere aerodrome near Chichester and met up with their pilot, Flight Lieutenant Farley.

Tangmere had a long history dating back to the Great War but now it was a base for Hawker Hurricanes as the Battle of Britain was well under way. As night flying of the fighter aircraft was not taking place, the base was being used at night for covert flights.

The storage space on the Lysander was very restricted but they managed to stow their equipment together with six sets of the latest design of W/T. These had been designed with an in-built aerial which could be used for reception and transmission for distances up to two hundred and fifty miles. This enabled short communications to be made without the risk of having to trail out a long aerial, which would however be necessary for a greater range.

In the briefing room Terry and his two agents sat in front of a large wall map and Farley explained the itinerary. First of all he went through the procedures in the event of an emergency landing, or if there was a need to bale out.

The flight would leave Tangmere just after dusk and cross the coast of occupied France at five hundred feet just west of Rouen. It would head due south passing well to the west of Paris. By the time the full moon had risen they would see the broad band of the slowly moving river Loire shining in the distance. The Lysander would then turn eastwards until the unmistakeable town of Blois appeared, straddling the river. This was their waypoint for turning due south towards Vichy France. The next waypoint was the thin sliver of the river Cher and the chosen landing ground was just two minutes flying time due south.

Vichy France had been chosen for the rendezvous because there was less security from the French administration and it was easy to cross into German-occupied territory. Terry had also told Sir Cedric that this would be the ideal location for his command centre, linking networks of circuits in both occupied and Vichy-controlled countryside.

As soon as it was dark they made their way out to the aeroplane. Terry chose to sit on the single forward-facing bench seat with his parachute tucked away beneath him, whilst his two thin companions sat together on the double seat facing him. Despite the lack of space he had insisted that they both wear their parachutes. It was impossible not to rub knees but they sat squashed in uncomfortable silence for the whole of the journey as speech was impossible above the sounds of the engine and slipstream.

They were met on landing by a group of French and Polish resistance members and hustled away to a hut in some woods several miles away. Terry sensed straight away friction between the French and the Poles. It was clear that the French resented the involvement of the Poles in the movement and did not trust them. Terry knew that his first job of leadership would be to establish trust between all of his agents.

The group made their way to the banks of the river Cher and crossed it in a small boat. The moonlight which had made their aircraft landing possible now worked against them as guards on either side of the river could easily have spotted them. However the Maquis, as the French resistance members called themselves, had done their reconnaissance well and chosen a narrow stretch of river on a bend where sightlines were very restricted.

The destination was a carefully concealed hideout in deep scrubland where the dense spikey bushes made access very difficult. It was this deep impenetrable thicket, or maquis which gave the resistance movement its name. Inside the redoubt Terry, Wren and Jay were introduced to Gilbert Renault, code name Rémy, the French resistance leader, and

Roman Czerniawski, or Pompey, the head of the Polish group.

After they had eaten and Terry had shared a bottle of Veterano with the partisans most of the groups went off to sleep in rough beds that lined the sides of the hideout. Terry, Rémy and Pompey however remained in deep discussion for the rest of the night, at the end of which they had agreed a strategy. Networks would be set up of French, British and Polish agents in both occupied and unoccupied territory whose objectives would be threefold; to intercept communications and assist in the breaking of German cyphers; to carry out sabotage to inhibit enemy troop movements and logistics, and to prepare a large programme of planning for an eventual liberation of the country.

The emphasis for the present would be on the first two objectives as the third was seen as a very distant prospect. The proposal for the new movement was forwarded to England for ratification by the British and Polish governments. Terry was established as Patrice Lefebre, a farm worker in a village near Blois and once agreement was given he started to establish circuits across the north of France.

Chapter 13
Betrayal

The British Government and the Polish and French Governments in Exile swiftly ratified the proposal and the Interallié networks as they were called were painstakingly built up over the next few months and by early 1941 were achieving considerable success. Acts of sabotage were carefully chosen as each successful attack on enemy forces was likely to be followed by reprisals in which suspected resistance members would be imprisoned and tortured. Communications interceptions were proving very useful to the British. Interallié were able to listen in to messages from remote parts of Germany not accessible to receivers in England. These were of course coded by Enigma and not understandable in France, but they were re-coded in the British WD code and forwarded to listening stations in East Anglia.

Then in early autumn of 1942 disaster struck. Three of the circuits in the Paris network were raided by the Gestapo and eighteen agents and partisans just disappeared. Just a week later another two circuits were broken up. Rémy and Terry were recalled to London and Rémy was asked to explain why he had not properly segregated the cells within his network of agents. His explanation was that he did not have sufficiently well-trained agents and that one of them had broken this cardinal rule. Terry was sent back by Lysander to take over what was left of the network and to re-build it.

This time however the journey did not go according to plan. When they arrived over the landing area there was no signal to guide them in. The pilot was circling the aircraft for a few minutes at about three hundred feet when it was suddenly attacked by a night fighter. The only indication was when the engine suddenly burst into flames in a flurry of cannon fire. The pilot immediately put the aircraft into a climb to gain height and instructed Terry to "Jump! Jump! Jump!"

The engine lost all power and the Lysander levelled off. Terry saw the pilot's cockpit canopy fly loose and get carried away in the slipstream. He pulled his own canopy emergency release and pushed it back. The slipstream caught it and it whirled away as he struggled to pull himself up and stand on the seat. In front of him the pilot had already emerged from the aircraft and, engulfed in flames, signalled Terry to get onto the ladder. He climbed over the lip of the fuselage and clambered clumsily down the ladder. The Lysander was now in a nose-down attitude and the ground approaching rapidly. He let go of the bottom rung and pulled the chute deployment ring at the same time.

No sooner had the chute snapped open than he saw the aircraft plummet past him and crash just below him. In the raging light of the flames he could just make out another parachute landing next to the wreckage and then he himself was crashing into thick foliage. Terry pulled himself to his feet and disentangled his parachute harness. Feeling his way across the scrub in the dim moonlight he came face to face with a figure dressed in black, holding a gun. Instinctively he drew his own gun and stood face to face with the other man, who he could now see was a German soldier. For a few seconds they stood frozen, and then simultaneously, they both threw their guns to the ground and just looked at each other. Terry could hear the approaching sounds of the rest of the German patrol so he waved at the soldier, and whispered "Schnell! Schnell!" They both grabbed their guns and ran off in opposite directions.

The following morning Terry was picked up by one of the partisans and taken to a new hideout. The original one had been discovered and destroyed. He was relieved to see that the Lysander pilot was already there and he recounted his extraordinary encounter with the German. He could not explain his behaviour but said that the soldier was little more than a boy and he could not bring himself to kill him.

The next day there was a sweep across the countryside by the Wehrmacht, looking for the occupants of the aircraft. Farms and villages were searched but the Maquis were well protected in their disguises as farm or office workers and the identity papers they used were not exposed as forgeries, owing to the skills of the craftsmen back in Section Fourteen.

Two days later it was a very different story. It was market day in the village near the farm where Terry worked outside Blois and he had taken the morning off for a short rendezvous with the head of one of his circuits. He was casually examining some cheeses on a stall when a nondescript man standing next to him said *"Pas de chiens aujourd'hui."* (No dogs around today.) This was a code for making contact in a town between agents who had not met before. In the country the phrase was *"Pas de lapins aujourd'hui."* (No rabbits).

Clam gave the correct response *"Non, il y a trop de bruit."* (No, it's too noisy.) The man set off along the market place and into a café, and Terry followed him. He assumed that his intended contact had been unable to come and had sent another in his place. However as he entered the café he was seized by two Gestapo officers who bundled him out of the door and into a car that had just drawn up. The car drove him to the Gestapo headquarters in Angers where he was put in a basement room which had been converted into a prison cell.

He sat on the edge of a wooden bench which was the only fitting in the room apart from a bucket in one corner, half full of excrement from a previous occupant. The fact that the correct code phrase had been used could only mean that one or more circuits had been compromised and that someone had talked. As he thought about his plight he ran his tongue around the hollow tooth containing the cyanide capsule. It was beginning to look as though he might have to use it.

He hadn't had time to dwell on this dismal option when the door to the cell was unlocked and two well-built men in shirt sleeves came in and set about systematically beating him about the face, arms and chest. Terry knew the technique. It was to beat and bruise the victim, possibly break a few bones, cause maximum pain but not put him at serious risk. Even as he thought about it, sure enough he felt his right cheekbone shatter. The men then left as quickly as they had entered. Terry knew that this was just the start.

The attack was repeated again that afternoon, the two men taking care to strike him on the existing wounds to intensify the pain. That evening he was taken from his cell to another room whose sole furniture was a heavy chair fixed to the ground and a woodstove. He was strapped into the chair and left alone for a few minutes until two men in Gestapo uniform entered. They took off their jackets and began interrogating him.

At first they just asked questions, but Terry stuck to his story of being Patrice Lefebre, a farm worker. So they started to go to work on his wounds, prodding them and striking his bruises with batons. Terry had heard about these two men from agents who had been tortured and released. The shorter of the two was known simply as Masuy, and was reputed to be the head of Gestapo interrogation, based in Paris. The taller man was Konrad Protz who was well known for his cruelty in the Angers prison and was hated by everyone in the region. His speciality was to brand swastikas onto the foreheads or arms of people he interrogated, even if they were perfectly innocent citizens that had been taken off the streets in random sweeps.

When it became clear that Terry was not going to talk, Protz said "It seems that you need a little more persuasion, which we can arrange." Suddenly he thrust his baton into Terry's mouth and jammed his jaw open. Masuy seized his head and held it tightly so he could not move it whilst his fellow henchman thrust his fingers into Terry's mouth and felt around for the hollow tooth. He carefully extracted the cyanide ampoule and threw it into the stove where it exploded and hissed. With that both men gathered up their belongings and left the room. Terry was taken back to his cell and flung onto the floor. He managed to crawl onto the bench but could not sleep because his injuries were too painful.

At around midnight he was seized again and taken back to the interrogation room and strapped into the chair. Protz was already there, standing next to the woodstove with a steel rod in his hand. "Have you slept well Herr Englander?" he asked in English. "Or have you had a chance to change your mind and tell me what I want to know?"

Terry shook his head pretending not to understand and Protz said "In that case we shall have to be a bit more persuasive" and he thrust the end of the steel rod into the depths of the fire. After half a minute or so he withdrew it and walked over to the chair, holding the rod with its white glowing end in front of him.

"Now we shall see what you have to say, or rather, you may not see very much after this" and he brought the gleaming end of the rod close to the front of the bound man's eyes. Terry instinctively strained his head away and clamped his eyes shut but there was no avoiding the searing heat. He felt his eyelids burn and sizzle as they curled and shrank. His left eye which was closest to the glowing rod started to blur then he passed out.

Chapter 14
Recovery

He regained consciousness in a doctor's surgery in Angers. His eyes were burning with agony and his head was wrapped in a heavy bandage. The doctor told him that his left eye was badly scorched and he was unlikely to see with it again. The lids of his eyes were almost burnt away but he thought the sight of the right eye could be saved as the surface had not been badly damaged.

The doctor told him that he had been found unconscious in a side street behind Gestapo headquarters and brought in by some passers-by. Terry would have to wear the bandages for a week and arrangements were being made to accommodate him in a sanatorium outside the town.

During the third night in the sanatorium he was visited by Thrush, the head of the Interallié Angers circuit, who he recognised from his voice. The partisans knew that the hospital was being watched and that Terry had been released in the hope of leading the Gestapo to other agents. Thrush had therefore entered the hospital by crossing the rooftops of the adjacent buildings.

He told Terry that the Tours circuit had been broken. One of the partisans had formed a liaison with another agent, a young women with whom he had been working. His wife had found out and reported him to the police who had told the Gestapo. He had broken under torture and revealed the names of the other circuit members, as well as codes and passwords. Thrush promised to help Terry return home as soon as his injuries had healed. Clam said he didn't want to go home, just to get back to work and seek revenge on his torturers.

A week later the doctor came to see him and closed the curtains over the window. He removed the bandages and assessed the damage. Even in the darkened room Terry winced as the light hit his unprotected eyes. His left eye was badly scarred and he could see only blurred shapes but the sight in his right eye was good, although he could not blink or close his badly shrunken eyelids. The doctor gave him a bottle of eye drops and told him to use them four times a day. He also gave him a patch for his left eye and a pair of very dark glasses to protect his good eye from the light.

That night Thrush returned and smuggled Terry across the rooftops to a safe house which was a farm outside Angers. There he met some of the partisans from Thrush's circuit. They pressed him to call in a Lysander to take him home but he was adamant. He was determined to take his revenge on Protz before getting back to work. He was told that Masuy was actually the code name of Georges Delfanne who was indeed the head of Gestapo interrogation but was based in Paris, only visiting other Gestapo offices as he needed. He was no longer in Angers.

Protz however was still very active and his movements were already being tracked by the Maquis. Because he liked to interrogate in the middle of the night his comings and goings were very erratic, but, paradoxically, being a religious man, he took Sundays off work. The one regular feature of his week was that he visited his mistress on Saturday evenings and stayed the night and all the following day, attending the village church. She lived in the village of

Montigné-les-Rairies, a few miles to the north of Angers, and Protz travelled by motorcycle to get there.

To Terry this was too good to be true. He wanted to lay an ambush right away. However Thrush and his colleagues were not at all enthralled by the idea. An assassination of Protz was bound to bring about massive reprisals. There had been too many already and the population were getting very hostile to the partisans and betrayals were on the increase.

So Terry bided his time. He needed several weeks for his eyes and other injuries to heal properly. His broken cheek had been crudely set by the doctor but was still extremely painful, especially when he tried to eat. His main consolation would have been his Veterano, but that was back at the farm near Blois which was too unsafe to visit, so he had to make do with Cognac of which a plentiful supply had been hidden from the invaders.

He spent the next few days reconnoitring the countryside around Angers and Montigné-les-Rairies, seeking a suitable place for an ambush. He found one on the narrow road that passed through a wooded area just before getting to the village. For most of its route through the woods the road was very straight, but just before emerging into open countryside again, the road made a double zig-zag around a small lake. Terry decided that this was the ideal place for an ambush and so he waited patiently for ten more days by which time his injuries were much improved.

The sight in his right eye was almost back to normal and the dark glasses compensated for his lack of eyelids. His left eye had improved slightly and he could make out most objects, albeit very blurred. In due course he tackled the subject of the ambush again with his colleagues. This time he had a well prepared plan which he convinced them would not bring retribution down on anyone.

The following Saturday was not suitable because the frequent road checkpoints would prove a problem. However Terry's research showed that the subsequent Saturday was ideal because there was a dance a few miles beyond Montigné in the village of La Flêche that night. Terry, Thrush and four other partisans travelled to Montigné in two combination motorbikes. They were stopped on the outskirts of Angers but their forged papers proved satisfactory and the excuse of the dance was accepted at face value as several other vehicles were heading the same way.

When they got to the wood they hid the combos behind some trees near the double bend. Thrush laid a stout cord across the road just on the left-hand bend and tied one end to a tree. He wrapped the other end half a turn around a tree on the opposite side of the road and waited. He kept the cord slack so that it lay on the ground in case any other traffic passed that way. Although Terry had determined that the road was little used at night they worried that the dance might attract a few more vehicles.

One of the partisans, Sparrow, walked back along the road onto the long straight stretch and stopped about a quarter of a mile away. He had a torch and waited to signal. The rest of the group hid in the trees on the right hand side of the road. One or two cars passed along the road but as it was by now almost dark the cord was not noticed.

After about half an hour and almost to the minute that Terry had estimated, the roar of a motorcycle engine could be heard approaching from the far end of the woods. As it entered the straight the engine opened up and the bike accelerated to top speed. When it sped past Sparrow he recognised the make and raised his torch to signal the letter 'V'. Thrush pulled the cord taut and raised it to about two feet off of the ground. The aim was to derail the bike but not to decapitate the rider.

Protz started to brake as he approached the left hand bend but when he saw the cord in his headlights he jammed on his brakes as hard as he could and started to swerve violently. The bike hit the cord and slewed sideways off the road, tumbled over several times and hit a tree. Protz was thrown off and landed in the scrub at the edge of the woods. As he struggled to his feet dazed and bruised, he was leapt upon by the three partisans who held him tight so that he could not move. Terry walked slowly up to the group and stood face to face with Protz so that the captive could see his disfigured face. "Herr Protz, you are about to die for your crimes." he said in German.

Scholtz gave a glimmer of recognition then sneered and said "If that is the case then all of you will shortly die too!"

"I don't think so," said Terry, you died in an unfortunate motorcycle accident. You really should not speed on these roads."

He then very slowly and deliberately put his hands on either side of Protz's head and pushed backwards. The Gestapo officer tried to struggle but was held fast by his captors. His eyes filled with fear as his head rotated inexorably backwards. Sykes had taught his pupil well. With a sickening crack Protz's spinal column snapped but Terry held his head steady and continued to push backwards. Suddenly Protz's heart began to race and flutter wildly but he remained conscious. The ancient Chinese certainly knew how to kill slowly.

On Terry's signal the partisans gently carried Protz over to a tree near the shattered motorcycle and carefully laid him next to it.

Terry said to him "Your neck is broken and your main nerve to the heart is stretched and damaged. It will take about twenty minutes for your heart to give out. I know you are a religious man. In that time, reflect on all the people you have tortured and killed."

With that the partisans started to coil up the cord and to make sure that there was no evidence of their presence. Terry inspected the zig-zag skid marks on the road. "Better than I could have hoped," he said to Thrush. "It will look as though he lost control on the bend and went into the trees. Now let's get to that dance so we have an alibi if any questions are asked!"

There were indeed questions asked and everyone who had attended the dance was grilled as whether they had seen anything on the road. The Gestapo interrogators got nowhere with their questions and eventually concluded that Protz' death was indeed an accident, so as Terry had hoped there were no repercussions. As a result of Protz's death he was replaced by another interrogator, no doubt equally ruthless, but honour had been satisfied.

Terry still rejected Thrush's exhortations to return to England. Thrush argued that he could not travel freely in France as his injuries would stick out like a sore thumb. However a couple of weeks later the decision was made for him and he received a message from Baker Street to fly back at the next full moon.

The Lysander drop-off and pick-up technique was now running quite smoothly and as his replacement and two more agents clambered down the ladder in the moonlight, Terry turned and said farewell to the partisans and then climbed aboard.

Chapter 15
Devastation

"Come in Clam. Glad to see you. My god, what's happened to your face?"

"Hello Sir Cedric, good to see you too. Just a little run-in with the Gestapo. Be sure they came off worst. So what's this all about?"

Attenby was half-hidden in his all-encompassing cloud of smoke.

"Sorry to have hauled you back at such short notice. With your face in that condition it's just as well. I'm afraid old chap we're going to have to start all over again.

"But start what all over again?"

"Poland dear boy, Poland. The SS have rolled up nearly all of our networks. One of your key agents talked and it went on from there. I can't blame him for caving in under the pressure but he should have bitten the pill before it got to that stage. No-one can withstand torture for long."

A deflated Terry slumped into a chair next to his boss. "Who was it? Who did they break? Which networks have gone?"

"It was Oyster. He was caught up in a general sweep but must have roused suspicion somehow because they let most of the others go and homed in on him. He held out for nearly a week before he cracked. He seems to have given them the names of all of the circuit heads because there were early morning raids and most of them were caught. Razorshell was out on a sabotage attack so they missed him but they took his family in, so he surrendered later to get them released. Fat chance. They shot them all as a warning to other partisans."

"Are any of the circuits left?" asked Terry.

"Yes, Mollusc and Spidercrab, but they've gone to ground. We're still not sure if they are compromised so they're having to wait it out. We need to rebuild as soon as we can. Things are hotting up in Poland with Sikorski agitating for a general uprising after Russia's victory at Stalingrad. He wants to oust Jerry before the Russians get there. We don't think he stands a chance but he's determined so we need all the intelligence and sabotage teams in place that we can get. But you'll have to start all over again."

"Well I'm right out of touch with the Polish situation," said Terry, "I've had my hands full in France. Have we any more agents ready here that speak the language?"

"No and that's the problem. We've exhausted the stock of Polish refugees in this country of any suitable material. However we have got lots of them flooding into Iraq and Persia and we're re-settling them as fast as we can in Egypt and Africa. The're in a pretty poor state. They've come from Siberia, where the Russians sent them after they invaded Poland."

"I doubt then if they're in any fit state to train as agents," said Terry, "besides, how will they get here?"

"Actually old boy, they won't. At least not to begin with. We'd like you to go out to the Middle East to give basic training to as many as you can find suitable.. Then send them back for final selection. Despite their ordeal many of them are just raring to get back at Jerry. You'll need a month in Palestine, a month in Cairo, another month in Rhodesia and then come home before you take them off to Poland. After his victory at Stalingrad Stalin will begin to roll up the Eastern Front and we want a network in place when he gets there."

"That's a bit of a tall order. Do I get any time at home? I haven't seen Vivien or Sarah for over a year."

"Just looking at you, I think I'm going to have to change the plan. You were supposed to start next month but I don't think we can send you out in that condition, you'd be too conspicuous. I think you should go and see someone the RAF have co-opted. Archie McIndoe specialises in rebuilding burnt faces and he'd love to get his scalpels on you. I'll arrange for you to see him tomorrow." With a bit of luck you'll be fit within a couple of months to set off. Meantime, go home now. Does Vivien know about your face?"

"No, and I'd rather she didn't but I really need to see her and the kid. So I'm going anyway. She'll have to get used to it."

"You're a cold fish to be sure. Archie will sort you out, he specialises in eyelids, you'll see."

Vivien was not as shocked as he expected at first, but he was wearing his dark glasses. He barely recognised little Sarah and she certainly didn't recognise him but then it had been a long time since they last saw each other. After the early euphoria of his return had settled down he took Vivien aside and explained about his injuries. She took off his glasses and looked deeply into his damaged eyes. She then gently kissed his face all over and murmured "scarring is only skin deep."

He asked about Rich and Doris and Vivien's face fell. "Doris died in childbirth six weeks ago. The baby too. He's shattered, doesn't know where to turn. It's only work that keeps him going."

"Oh god no! Poor Rich! I must go and see him. This is appalling."

Vivien said "He's living in Rickmansworth now, working at Radlett for Handley Page. I'll take you on the bus."

"No," said Terry, "I'll go on the bike. I was ok coming here, the goggles protect my eyes and I can see fine out of my good eye."

"Well you be careful. You really ought to have a car, it can't be safe on two wheels with poor eyesight. Rich has got himself a little Morris. He and Doris used to come over and take me and Sarah out on Sundays."

Rich was as depressed as Vivien had said, and was dreading the approaching Christmas without Doris. Terry tried all he could to cheer him up and invited him to spend Christmas with him and Vivien.

His appointment next day was at Queen Victoria Hospital in Sussex with Archibald McIndoe who expertly assessed him and said "You need four new eyelids, which is not a problem. I see you have tough arms, can you afford to lose some skin?" McIndoe went on to explain that he intended to graft skin from his upper arms onto his face. To do this however, he needed to stitch his arm to his face for ten days and then cut away the grafted skin to shape new eyelids. The muscles in the remaining shreds of his eyelids would enable the new tissue to blink over the eyes.

Terry Sexton was admitted that day and the first operation carried out that evening. McIndoe could only do one side at a time and Terry would have to hold his arm over his head for the ten days. I wooden splint was strapped to his back to carry the weight.

On the ward there were a very strange array of patients; some with heavily bandaged faces, others with arms or legs grafted to their face or hands. The ten days passed very slowly but then he went into the operating theatre once more. When he recovered from the anaesthetic he found a bandage over the wound on the arm from where the graft had been taken, and that his left eye was covered in a dressing. Archie told him that all had gone well and that in three days the eye dressing would come off, and he would have rudimentary eyelids. He warned that more surgery would be required. Terry would have the Christmas period to recover and then McIndoe would repeat the graft with the right arm and eye.

Terry demurred. He said that he had an important tour of duty coming up and could he defer the second operation until he got back? McIndoe replied that he could, but that every week that went by without the benefit of blinking his eye, would lead to further deterioration of his sight.

When the dressing came off his left eye he was surprised at how realistic the eyelids looked. They did not have lashes, but he was able to blink them and feel the moisture on the surface of the eye for the first time since the torture. McIndoe was pleased with the result but said that he needed to do another operation on the lids to trim them so that they closed properly.

Rich spent the Christmas holiday with Terry and his family and they did their best to keep him cheerful. He loved to play with little Sarah but she was also a constant reminder of the child he had lost. The wartime Christmas was very short and Rich went back home to start work for the last few days of the year. At the same time Archie McIndoe had arranged for Terry's badly fractured cheekbone to be reset by another surgeon Harry Gillies at a hospital in Basingstoke so when he came home for the New Year his face was a mass of bandages once more.

After New Year the bandages were removed and to his great pleasure, his rugged features were symmetrical once more. A week later Terry was re-admitted to hospital and Archie McIndoe repeated the graft for his right eye.

There then followed a month of more minor surgery to reshape his eyelids and to graft fresh skin over his forehead which had also been badly scorched. The only noticeable peculiarity was the lack of eyelashes but this was a minor issue.

At the end of March he went to see Sir Cedric and declare himself ready for duty. Cedric was impressed by his new face. "Jove Clam, you look better than you ever did before! I must go and see Archie, I am getting a bit worn round the edges myself!"

"What's the programme then?" said Terry. "Are we ready to go?"

"Not just yet. Bill Fairbairn is coming back from Canada to go with you and there are two more instructors going along as well. We can go in three days time if his flight gets in as scheduled. You should be well equipped to sort out some of the wheat from the chaff. There is however one pleasant duty I have to perform. For this exercise you will travel as an army officer, and you have been given a promotion with a temporary commission as Lieutenant. Congratulations Lieutenant Terence Patrick Sexton."

Three days later Terry collected together some personal items and tropical clothing and set off for Brize Norton airfield. On arriving he met up again with Bill Fairbairn, Sergeant-Major Alan Trufford and Sergeant Brian Greatchild, the instructors who were to go with him. In the Control Tower briefing room they were given instructions by Freddie Younge who had come to see them off.

"It's a night flight to Gibraltar first, with a brief stayover during the day, then another night flight to Cairo. Then it is just a short flip across to Lydda airbase in Palestine. You'll be met and taken to the Polish refugee camp where you can start your interviews. The military are already interviewing men who want to join the Polish Army in Exile and they're swamped with volunteers. They will pass over to you anyone who looks likely material. Anything I've missed?"

"No, I expect we'll muddle through, won't we chaps/" They nodded in agreement.

They climbed aboard the new Liberator aircraft that Transport Command had on lease from America, and on a chilly evening in the middle of April 1943 they set off on the first leg of their flight. The route took them across the Bay of Biscay then around the west coast of Spain and Portugal, out of range of the radio direction finding stations that Spain used to monitor the coast. Whilst Spain was supposedly neutral it was known that they fed such information back to the Germans in France.

The bomb bay of the aircraft had been fitted with mattresses so they were able to get a few hours sleep but as they were wearing life jackets it was rather uncomfortable.

The aircraft landed just after seven o'clock in the morning and a car took them to the Convent, the residence of the Governor of Gibraltar, who introduced himself as Major-General Mason-Macfarlane who had succeeded Sir Edmund Ironside. He invited them for breakfast but did not ask who they were or what their mission was. Being too canny a Scot to probe, he offered them a car to go into the town for the day before their evening departure.

Terry took the opportunity to visit a duty-free shop and purchase a couple of cases of Veterano brandy that had been smuggled into Gibraltar from Algeciras. He had missed his favourite tipple over the last two years and seized the chance whilst he had it.

Night fell rapidly as the party boarded the aircraft once again that evening. Just before the entrance hatch was closed an additional three passengers boarded for the trip to Cairo but the two groups kept entirely to themselves, as Sexton settled down for a restless sleep.

The flight across North Africa was a pleasant difference to the first leg as the skies were clear of enemy aircraft and the Allied anti-aircraft guns held their fire. Cairo airfield was a bustling hive of activity with aircraft arriving and leaving from all parts of the British Empire at war.

Sexton and his party were taken to a hut some distance away from the main buildings and given breakfast. The other passengers from the flight disappeared just as suddenly as they had arrived. An hour later a jeep arrived to take them to a parked Dakota painted in army camouflage. It was a regular flight between Cairo and Lydda, which had just been renamed from its former title of Wilhelma Airfield.

It was just a short three-hour flight to Palestine and they were met by a young Major from Army Intelligence who took them to a barracks just adjacent to the airfield. He explained that the Polish refugee camp was further north at Hedera, out in the desert. There were about five thousand refugees and they had arrived in a very poor state after a long ordeal of a journey from Siberia via Persia, with sickness and disease rife amongst the children.

Major Fletcher told Sexton that the army had been swamped with Polish volunteers from the camp to fight back at the enemy. The news had just come through of the total destruction of the Ghetto in Warsaw by German troops. Thousands of Polish Jews had been killed or deported to Treblinka concentration camp. Revenge was in the air and Fletcher had singled out fifteen volunteers who he thought might be agent material and arranged for Terry to interview them next day.

During the following few days Sexton whittled the volunteers down to eleven and the next three weeks were taken up giving them basic training in fieldcraft and unarmed combat.

Terry and his colleagues spent the evenings mingling with the soldiers at the barracks and sharing grubby cigarettes and Veterano with Major Fletcher.

At the end of the month there were just nine remaining candidates considered suitable to be trained as agents. Before being sent back to England they were given the opportunity to say goodbye to their families. The Polish refugees in the camp were soon to be relocated to communities in Rhodesia and South Africa whose governments had agreed to the re-settlement until Poland was freed once more. The volunteers and Sexton's training group boarded a Dakota and flew back to Cairo. A Liberator was waiting to take the new recruits back to England where Freddie Younge was arranging to complete their training.

Sexton and his group however had to start again with more selections, this time from the refugee camps in Egypt. There were several thousand Poles in these camps situated around Cairo. They had been given a contact in Cairo, Major Stanislaw Olszewski who was responsible for identifying candidates from the refugees for Polish Army and Air Force training. Once again there were plenty of volunteers and over the next three weeks twenty-one people were selected, including three women with outstanding potential. The rest of the refugees would not be staying much longer in the camps as they were due to be relocated in South Africa and Rhodesia where there was a growing community of refugee Poles.

Chapter 16
Reconstruction

Terry and Olszewski hit it off right away and he was invited to visit Heliopolis Air Base on the outskirts of Cairo. Stanislaw told him in confidence that he was shortly to become commander of an air training school there for teenagers from amongst the refugees. He had been appointed to this post by General Sikorski himself. The air base was very new and as yet had no trainees, only about twenty officers who were busy organising the facilities in readiness for the opening later in the year. The only movements were occasional training flights from other air bases.

Terry began his round of interviews whilst Fairbairn, Trufford and Greatchild started instructing those that had passed the preliminary selection. In the evenings the group mingled with the other base staff in the Officers Mess. One of these, Vladimir Stepanov, was a Russian citizen who had come across with the refugees as a guide, and decided to join the Polish forces. His English language was almost non-existent and his Polish was almost as bad. Sexton was able to brush up on his Russian as they chatted and learnt a great deal about the activities on the Russian front. He was careful to be discreet about his own activities in case Stepanov was an agent planted by the Russians.

About three weeks into the recruitment campaign Stanislaw invited Terry and his group to a dance in the station officers' mess that evening. A number of young women from one of the refugee camps had been invited, one of whom was Stanislaw's girl friend Dorota. At about five o'clock that evening an ancient Avro Anson landed at the field. It was on a navigation training flight from Hillside airfield in Rhodesia and had seven British trainee navigators on board. It was too late for the return flight so the crew and trainees were billeted on the station for the night and invited to the dance.

The dance was about to begin when Olszewski sprang a big surprise on the assembled company. He told them that a Liberator had just arrived from Gibraltar and that the Polish Prime Minister in Exile General Sikorski was on board and that he would be coming to speak to everyone. He was on a tour of Polish servicemen and refugees in the Middle East and was starting in Cairo.

A few minutes later the General arrived with his entourage, which included his daughter, Madame Zofia Lesniowska. He gave a very powerful speech saying how well the war was going, that the tide was turning and soon Poland would be free once again. He congratulated Major Olszewski on the progress made in establishing the training centre and rewarded him by awarding him the Virtuti Militari for his work.

After his speech which ended in thunderous applause and table banging, the Prime Minister insisted on touring the tables around the dance floor. He was well shielded by his Adjutant and a group of burly guards but walked around talking to the guests, as did his daughter who worked the room in the opposite direction.

At one of the tables two of the trainee navigators from the Anson and Terry Sexton were talking to some of the Polish women. Vladimir Stepanov was also with them, and being very charming to the women. One of the airmen Bill Dawson, was much taken by one of the refugees, a beautiful Polish girl, Sylwia Baranska and asked her to dance. When she stood up she was a statuesque five foot ten inches, but Bill was only five feet six tall. However she was not at all bothered by the height difference and caught him to her in a tight hold as they danced around the floor.

Bill was from the north of England with a broad Geordie accent. He had a very distinctive Mallen streak of white hair flopping across his face, which Sylwia fondly brushed back as she smiled sweetly at him. She told him about her home in Poland and the ordeal of her transfer to a Russian prison camp and subsequent transfer to Persia and then Cairo. She said that in Poland her father had been a diplomat and that she was a friend of Zofia Lesniowska and hoped to talk to her later.

When they returned to their table as the music ended, Zofia was already there having seen Sylwia get up to dance. She was shocked to see that Sylwia and her parents were now refugees with nowhere to go. Sylwia reassured her that they were scheduled to be re-located in Rhodesia or South Africa and that all would be well.

Terry, Bill and his colleagues were introduced to Zofia and they were soon joined by the General himself and Major Olszewski. The General was very pleased to see Terry again and asked what he was doing in Cairo. Terry spoke in very general terms about helping to re-settle the refugees because Stepanov was listening intently. Sikorski thanked the British contingent for their support for Poland in its time of distress. He turned to Stepanov to thank him in very stilted Russian for bringing the refugees out of Siberia. Terry stepped in and translated because whilst Sikorski had studied Russian at school, it was very limited.

When Stepanov got up to dance with one of the Polish women, Terry told Sikorski about his real mission. As the evening drew on Sikorski and his daughter left for their quarters but the rest of the General's group stayed on. The pilot and co-pilot of the General's Liberator came across to talk to the British airmen.

The pilot's name was Flight Lieutenant Mak Prchal and he was a Czech of immense flying experience. He had been piloting Sikorski for over two years. His co-pilot was a British officer, a Scott, Squadron Jock Leader Haydock, known to his friends as 'Jockey', an allusion to the Lancashire racecourse. Bill Dawson questioned them closely about their aircraft as he was scheduled to fly Liberators after he had completed his navigation training. Jockey admitted not to have much experience on the type but Mak Prchal waxed lyrical about the ease of handling and invited Bill to look over the aircraft the next day before he flew back to Rhodesia on his navigation exercise.

The next morning Sexton and his recruitment team had breakfast with Sikorski and Zofia Lesniowska who were due to spend ten days on a tour of the Polish refugee camps in Egypt before setting off for their next stop in Persia. Terry told them that he was to leave in a couple of days' time to go to Rhodesia to recruit more agents from the Polish refugees there and the General wished him and his party well, before going for his flight.

Two days later Sexton loaded another group of prospective agents onto a Liberator at Lydda and despatched them back to England. The following day Terry and his group climbed inside a Dakota for the flight to Bulawayo in Southern Rhodesia. There was one refuelling stop in Uganda and then the aircraft arrived at Hillside airfield where they were met by the officer in charge of the re-settlement programme, Nikodem Krakowski from the Polish Consulate in Salisbury.

There were two main settlement camps around Salisbury, at Marandelias and Rusape and more camps in Northern Rhodesia. After Sexton's delegation had settled into their accommodation they talked to Krakowski about their programme. He told them that when refugees first arrived they were taken to one or other of the camps, but that his job was to see that they were re-settled with Southern and Northern Rhodesian families as soon as possible. This was made possible by funding from the Polish Government in Exile in London. He said that if they wanted to recruit quickly they should visit the camps as the re-settled refugees were widely spread and it would require a great deal of travelling.

Bill Fairbairn was anxious to get back to Canada and Sexton wanted to return to England to start inserting covert agents back into Poland and re-establish his networks there. It was decided that they would spend two weeks selecting and training agents in Salisbury and then return home to England. There were refugees arriving every day from Persia and Egypt but the camps in Northern Rhodesia were not yet ready to receive them so there was little point in spending time there.

Out on the airfield at Hillside next to the Dakota there were a number of Avro Anson and Harvard aircraft neatly parked in rows in the dispersal area. A group of trainees were inspecting the Dakota and amongst them, Bill Dawson was quizzing the pilot about its controls. He told him that he was training as a navigator on the Ansons and Harvards and that once his training was finished later in the year he was due to join a new squadron equipped with Liberators. He was also hoping to be given a temporary Commission. Whilst they were talking another Dakota arrived from Lydda and started to disembark Polish refugees who were being met by Nikodem Krakowski.

Krakowski had arranged transport to the camps and Sexton's group were taken in a shooting brake to Rusape where they started their sifting of possible candidates. As before the Polish refugees were very keen to contribute to the war effort and several likely prospects were identified. A week later they returned to Hillside with the short-listed candidates and Fairbairn, Trufford and Greatchild started more in-depth training whilst Sexton prepared to visit Marandelias Camp.

That evening they dined in the mess hall at the airbase and Bill Dawson came across to see them, in high spirits. That day a Dakota had arrived with more refugees from Cairo. Amongst them he had spotted Sylwia Baranska and had been able to have a short chat. She was being sent to Marandelias and Bill had promised to visit her there on his next day's leave.

Terry Sexton took the shooting brake to Marandelias and started interviewing once more. He did not see Sylwia at all

119

whilst he was there as he was too busy but he did bump into Bill Dawson on the third evening, who had switched some leave with another trainee and driven across to see her.

At the end of the week Sexton returned to Hillside with seven prospective agents and met up with his training group. Work with the trainees from Rusape had gone well with only one of them proving unsuitable for the role. The successful ones were sent to Cairo to be forwarded to London with Bill Fairbairn who had got agreement to his leaving early to return to Canada. The new recruits from Marandelias camp were handed over to Alan Trufford and Brian Greatchild to continue their training in combat and fieldcraft whilst Terry Sexton gave them lessons in Morse code and wireless telegraphy.

Three days before they were all due to leave for home, Sexton got an urgent top secret message to return to London via Gibraltar. A Bombay bomber was on its way to pick him up and would fly direct to Gibraltar via Nigeria. He was to report to the Governor on his arrival. His journey was to remain completely secret.

The Bombay arrived later that evening and was immediately surrounded by a crowd of eager airmen who rarely saw such craft on the training airbase. Terry casually strolled over to join the group and had a quiet word with the pilot, explaining that he was the passenger for the flight. He turned to go back to his room to prepare for his journey when he was collared by a very excited Bill Dawson.

"Lieutenant! I'm so glad to see you! I have some wonderful news. Sylwia and I are getting married!"

"What's that!" said Terry, "That's fast work! When's the happy day?"

"Oh, not soon I'm afraid. I'm not allowed to marry out here as a trainee, but when I get my Commission, then we can. I know it's been quick, but we've seen each other several times these last two weeks and we're both quite sure! Sylwia is being relocated with a family in Livingstone, just across the border in Northern Rhodesia. It's not too long a journey on my leave days."

"Well I'm very happy for you both. I could see a spark between you at the dance in Cairo but didn't realise it would come to this. Wartime romances are all the rage at the moment, so make the most of your time. You'll eventually get posted you know."

"Of course I will" said Bill, "but it won't make any difference. We'll be together after the war, that's all that matters."

Back in his room Terry pondered over his orders again. He was to remain on the aircraft until it arrived in Gibraltar. He was to board the Bombay under cover of darkness and the Hillside Warrant Officer would take him to the aircraft. The flight to Nigeria would take place during the night and the aircraft would refuel and stay on the ground during the day, and fly up to Morocco again in darkness. There Terry would transfer to a Dakota that would fly across the Straits to Gibraltar, again arriving in darkness. The Governor's adjutant would meet him at the aircraft and take him straight to the Convent. His presence there was to be on a strictly 'need to know' basis only.

Dusk fell promptly at about six pm and Warrant Officer Jackson, who also doubled as a flying instructor came to collect Terry. He was ushered into a shooting brake and told to lie low in the seat.

Jackson told him that only the captain of the crew knew of his presence on the aircraft and so climbing aboard was difficult because it had to be through the bomb doors. A hammock was slung across the bomb bay and he climbed clumsily into it as the doors closed underneath him. A rack close to his head had some thermos flasks and boxes of victuals for his journey. Another rack near his feet contained glass bottles and pots which were his crude toilet facilities.

The aircraft was eventually airborne and shook its way north-westwards towards Nigeria with cold air blasting in from hidden cracks and crannies, giving Terry little opportunity to sleep. He knew nothing of the stopover in Nigeria as he stayed on board all during the long day. The heat was stifling and, in contrast to the night flight, there was no movement of air at all inside the fuselage. He heard the sounds of aircrew moving around outside and the heat and the smell of fuel being loaded made him physically sick, which just added to the stifling atmosphere inside the aircraft.

Eventually the external noises faded away and he managed to doze off. He was woken by the sounds of the crew returning and before long the Bombay was rattling down the runway and into the air. This next leg of the flight was the most dangerous as it had to route over the sea around the bulge of French West Africa. Whilst the more direct route over French Equatorial Africa to Libya would have been shorter the instructions were to avoid overflying anywhere that could compromise the mission were the aircraft to fall into unknown hands.

The flight arrived in Casablanca before dawn with a terrifying landing in a strong buffeting cross-wind for which the airfield was notorious. Once the crew had departed a British security officer arrived to help Terry climb out of his hammock. He was stiff and bruised from head to toe and stumbled out onto the red-hot tarmac. The officer took him by car to a hut at the side of the dispersal pan and inside were a change of clean clothing and a hastily-improvised shower consisting of an overhead barrel of water and a hosepipe. There was also an armchair, food and drink and some English newspapers, several days out of date. The officer explained to Terry that there was an aircraft waiting to take him to Gibraltar but that it couldn't leave until after dark.

He left and Terry immediately stripped and showered. Helping himself to some food and several glasses of Veterano from his satchel, he settled down to read the newspapers. At six pm the officer returned and took Terry to a waiting Dakota. As before he had to go through the cloak and dagger process of being smuggled on board without being seen by crew or observers. Casablanca was a nest of spies and double-agents for every nationality conceivable and each aircraft movement was monitored, hence a strict security screen which kept members of the public over a mile away from the aircraft. Despite this it was well known that the airfield ground crews probably harboured agents so Terry's complicated routine was considered essential.

The inside of the Dakota was divided into sections separated by curtains and Terry was taken to a section forward of the door at the rear of the fuselage. He could hear the rustling of papers in the section in front of him so he knew that others were on board. After the curtain behind him had been drawn he heard whispers as someone else was ushered into the rearmost section. The windows of the aircraft were blocked off by plywood screens so the comings and goings outside could not be seen. The aircrew must have been aboard already as the engines started almost immediately and the Dakota began to taxi shortly afterwards.

The trip to Gibraltar across the straits was mercifully short and the landing uneventful. the passengers in the Dakota were unloaded in reverse order. First Terry heard the people in the rear compartment leave, and then after a decent interval a tall man pushed past the rear curtain and signalled Terry to follow him. Once in the car the man introduced himself as Flight Lieutenant Perry, adjutant to the Governor of Gibraltar. They were soon at the Convent and Perry took Terry immediately to the Governor's study where Major-General Mason-Macfarlane was waiting for him. Perry took Terry's belongings to his room and promised to return later to show him his accommodation.

Macfarlane greeted Sexton warmly and they chatted for a few moments before Macfarlane said "You know, you are a bit of a legend on the Rock amongst those who know, after your exploit swimming across from Algeciras. No one believes it could be done. In fact we have here a specialist in underwater bomb disposal who would dearly like to get his hands on you. We have a major problem here. There is an

Italian consulate building in Algeciras with an underwater entrance, and they send out teams to fix mines to the bottoms of our ships. Commander Crab, 'Buster', and his team go out every day to remove them, but we're still losing about two ships a month."

"I'm afraid I'm already fully committed elsewhere," said Terry, "besides, I've had enough underwater experience to last a lifetime."

"I know," said Macfarlane, "and anyway, I have further uses for you. I'm not just a housekeeper here in Gib. Confidentially, I am Head of Naval Intelligence here in the Med. Early next year I'm going back to England to head up all intelligence and to prepare for the invasion. I will be your new boss, so I don't want you wasted splashing around in the Med defusing fireworks."

" Now, I suppose you know why you're here, don't you?"

"I haven't got a clue! I was just told to get here post-haste and report to you!" Sexton replied.

"Good. At least our security is holding. The situation is this. The Polish Government in Exile is split over the issue of the Katyn massacres. General Sikorski is trying to pull all the factions together and patch things up with the Russians. Churchill and Stalin have agreed that Sikorski and Ivan Maisky the Russian Foreign Minister should meet here in secret to sort it out. If General Anders gets to hear about it there will be war inside the Polish Government so it has to be absolutely top secret. Sikorski is on his way back from the Middle East and he has specifically asked that you be here to act as his translator."

Chapter 17
Gibraltar Again

The flight from Cairo was uneventful, unlike the journeys taken before the victory at el Alemein. Before being allocated to General Sikorski's detail Mak Prchal had flown Churchill from Cairo to Gibraltar in an Avro York prior to the battle. The journey along the North African coast had been perilous. Over the British-held territory the airspace was controlled by the Allies but on leaving the safety of this zone, the aircraft had to move out over the Mediterranean with fighter aircraft as escort. Because of their limited range the fighters had eventually to turn back, leaving the unarmed York to lumber on alone.

On this occasion however the whole of the North African coast was in Allied hands and Prchal could safely fly General Sikorski's Liberator over land for the whole route until it was time to turn north-west towards the Rock. As they started to make landing preparations Prchal asked the co-pilot to do the pre-landing checks. Jockey Haydock had only had a few hours on Liberators and had been captain for only one landing.

The weather was very clear and Gibraltar could be seen many miles ahead. There was a westerly wind so they could do a straight-in approach from the east. Haydock took out the check list and ran through the many switch changes and checks required before making the approach. Eventually Prchal lined the aircraft up with the runway from about ten miles out. At five miles he throttled back slightly and called "Flaps, Stage one", and Haydock moved the flap control down one step. At three miles Prchal called "Flaps Stage two." And Haydock then lowered full flap.

Two miles out and Prchal called "Gear down.' Haydock reached for the undercarriage lever but Prchal interjected "Brakes off first". Haydock reached across the control console to the parking brake lever and released it, then lowered the undercarriage. "mustn't forget the brakes!" reproved Prchal.

During flight the wheel brakes were held stationary by applying the parking brake, to prevent undue vibration from rotating wheels. The procedure during take-off was, first of all to ensure that the aircraft was climbing. Then the wheel brakes would be applied to stop the rotation and the parking brake applied. The undercarriage would then be retracted. This served two purposes. It prevented dust, water or mud from the wheels being thrown around in the undercarriage bay, but, more importantly, it prevented the gyroscopic forces of the rotating wheels from upsetting the control of the aircraft. It was clearly important to make sure that the parking brake was taken off again before the aircraft touched down.

The landing was uneventful and the Liberator was guided to a parking spot close to a set of huts. Two army jeeps came out to meet them and armed guards leapt out and immediately surrounded the aircraft. After a few minutes the hatch of the aircraft was opened and General Sikorski and his party emerged. They were quickly hustled into the nearest hut where they were greeted by the Station Commander, Group Captain Bolland and the Governor of

Gibraltar, Lieutenant-General Mason-Macfarlane. After greetings and introductions the party moved to a fleet of cars which sped them to Government House, the Convent, outside the perimeter of the airfield. General Sikorski and his party were housed in the guest apartments at the east end of the building.

The guests had some time to freshen up and then, at the request of General Sikorski's daughter Madame Zofia Lesniowska, several of them went by car into Gibraltar town for a shopping expedition. They came back with many packages of duty-free goods, including suspiciously clinking cases. The acquisitions were sent ahead to the airfield to be loaded into the Liberator.

After the guests had taken time to rest and change they assembled for dinner in the dining room of the Convent. By the time the meal was finished it was close to midnight and most of the party retired for the night. As his Adjutant Adam Kulakowski was about to go, Sikorski summoned him. "Adam, I've left my briefcase in the aircraft with the medals in it. I know it's late, but if the Governor will provide a car, would you please go and retrieve it."

Macfarlane immediately summoned a car and Kulakowski set off back to the airfield whilst Sikorski and Macfarlane retired to the Governors' office and shut the door. As they sat down, Macfarlane said "It is confirmed. I had a call this evening to say that Maisky will arrive about six tomorrow morning.. We are very tight on accommodation but I'm putting his party in my accommodation in the west wing. My wife and I are staying with friends in town. We will come back to give them breakfast at about seven thirty and then go into town on a pretext for a meeting in the government offices. I cannot be here when you meet."

"Where are we to stay whilst Maisky and his party are in the house?"

"I am afraid I must ask you all to stay in your rooms until they have left. Breakfast will be served in your rooms at about eight. I will have the library kept under guard and Lieutenant Sexton will collect you General, from your room at about nine and take you there for the meeting as you cannot use any other room in case anyone sees you or Maisky. We will arrange for him to leave later in the morning, but your party must stay in your rooms until he has left."

"Thank you Governor, I am most grateful that you are doing this for us. The Prime Minister spoke directly to Stalin to arrange this meeting and none of my staff know about it, or will know. The situation is very delicate. Half of my Cabinet are violently opposed to any contact with the Soviet Union after the Katyn massacre and I must persuade them very quickly to come around. General Anders is leading the opposition and I have to work on him. This meeting with Maisky may give me the opportunity to do so. Tell me, is Lieutenant Sexton here yet?"

"Yes General, he is in the next room. No-one else knows he is here and it must be kept secret. If it becomes known that the British Secret Service are involved it would have dire consequences for the Allies. Shall I call him in?"

"Yes of course, we are old friends." Macfarlane went to the door and called Terry Sexton to join them.

"Ześć znowu General!" greeted Terry. "Ześć Lieutenant!" replied Sikorski. "It is good to see you old friend, it has been too long! What have you been doing since I saw you last?"

"I've just returned from Rhodesia, doing the same thing as when we met up in Cairo, training Polish agents. I did get a chance to meet up with some of our Polish exile friends living in camps around Salisbury. Is Madame Zofia with you? I'd like to see her again. I have a message for her about Sylwia Baranska. She and Bill Dawson are to be married."

"Yes, Zofia is here but she has gone to bed. I do not think she should know you are here, but I will give her the news. Now, I am sure that Lieutenant-General Macfarlane can find us some good Scotch whisky to toast our re-union!"

After half an hour or so reminiscing, there was a knock on the door and Adam Kulakowski entered and gave Sikorski his briefcase. As he was about to leave, Sikorski said "One moment Lieutenant Kulakowski, I would like a word with you and Lieutenant Sexton here."

He bent down and opened his briefcase and took out a bottle of Polish vodka, and two maroon leather-covered boxes. He laid the boxes on the desk and opened the lids.

"Lieutenant Kulakowski and Lieutenant Sexton. You have both served Poland well beyond the call of duty. You have faced danger from the enemy outside and from traitors within and have been tortured and imprisoned. It is my solemn duty and great personal pleasure to bestow on you the highest award possible for military honour."

Taking a ribboned medal from one of the boxes and placing it around Kulakowski's neck he intoned

"Lieutenant Adam Kulakowski, I award you the Virtuti Militari, Fifth Class, for outstanding services to the Polish nation."

And taking a similar medal from the other box he placed it around Terry's neck saying

"Lieutenant Terence Sexton, I award you the Virtuti Militari, Fifth Class, for outstanding services to the Polish nation.

I give these decorations in recognition of the great services you have both rendered to the common cause and the attainment of final and decisive victory, animated as you have always been by profound friendship for Poland and for Polish soldiers, sailors and airmen.

And now, whilst we have enjoyed the Governor's whisky, let us celebrate with him, a glass or two of genuine Polish vodka, for which forethought Adam, I believe we owe you our thanks!"

Chapter 18
Maisky and Sikorski

Ivan Maisky arrived by another Liberator aircraft at about half past six the next morning. The flight had been bumpy and his party had not slept well. Macfarlane met the team at the airport and escorted them to the Convent where they were installed in the Governor's private rooms at the west end of the building.

At about nine o'clock Terry called at Maisky's room, which was guarded by two Russian officers. He introduced himself as one of the adjutants to Macfarlane and asked to speak to Maisky. He was searched and then ushered into the suite. Maisky was just finishing breakfast with Macfarlane and Terry introduced himself as Lieutenant Bradshaw, one of the adjutants to the Gibraltar Governor. "If you are ready, Comrade Maisky, I will take you to the library. The guards are making sure that no one sees us."

They made their way along a short corridor and entered the library which was guarded by two British officers. Sexton ushered Maisky and his adjutant into the room then left by another door on the opposite side of the room. He went then to fetch General Sikorski from his room in the east wing and escorted him into the library by the second door, thus ensuring that no-one knew that the two diplomats were in the same room.

Terry began "As you are aware, Lieutenant General Mason-Macfarlane must not be present at this meeting, which has been arranged in the greatest secrecy. Only he, the Prime

Minister Winston Churchill, Marshall Stalin and the four of us in this room know that it is taking place." We offer this facility so that the Polish Government in London and the Government of the Soviet Union can discuss their differences with a view to reconciliation and re-establishment of Diplomatic Relations."

Maisky responded politely "Lieutenant Bradshaw we are most grateful for this opportunity so please pass our thanks to Lieutenant General Mason-Macfarlane." After introducing his own adjutant, Maisky turned to Sikorski and said "Comrade General, It is a long time since we last met on a happier occasion. I am pleased that you have agreed to this meeting. I understand the pressures you are under as a leader in exile with no means of exercising power."

"Comrade Maisky. I am a soldier. I fought wars for my political masters. But now I have no political masters. I have been thrust into the role of Prime Minister of the Polish government. As a soldier, I abhor the crimes committed against twenty thousand Polish officers. I want that crime avenged. Joseph Stalin is the perpetrator of that crime, and Major-General Blokhin the executioner.

However, now, as a politician, my prime objective is to defeat Germany and free Poland for its citizens, and this is what Prime Minister Churchill has pledged to me. The Soviet Union, Britain and the United States are Allies to defeat Germany. My small Polish forces are also part of that alliance. Therefore, with great reluctance, I accept that the Polish Government and the Soviet Union must work together and therefore I agree to work to ensure that members of my government accept this decision."

Maisky listened to this speech with a look of disdain upon his face. He turned to his adjutant and muttered a few words to him in Russian. His adjutant responded in muted tones and then Maisky turned to the General and keeping a straight face he replied "Comrade General, my Government denies all knowledge of this senseless massacre of Polish officers. The evidence points conclusively to this act being perpetrated by the German army when they maliciously attacked the Soviet Union through Polish territory in June 1941. My Government also does not recognise the small group of Polish refugees in London who claim to be a government."

At this, Sikorski gasped and started to respond, but Maisky continued "However, in the spirit of reconciliation we are prepared to instigate an investigation into the truth or falsity of the perpetrators of the unfortunate Katyn deaths, and have, without prejudice, suspended from office Major-General Blokhin, pending these inquiries. Furthermore, my Government is prepared to offer limited recognition to the group of Polish exiles in London who are usefully deploying former Polish troops and airmen on the side of the Allies, and who recognise you as their leader. However, we do have one condition. General Anders is proving intransigent in his opposition to any co-operation between our respective govern – er – organisations. We require that he be removed immediately. Other than that, I would like to shake your hand on our reconciliation." Maisky held out his right hand.

General Sikorski declined his hand saying "The documents found on the bodies of the Polish officers all pre-date the June 1941 offensive. There are no documents dating from after the treacherous Soviet Union invasion of Poland in

1939. Regarding my Government, I cannot do as you request and I am sure you understand why. General Anders will remain on my staff. Winston Churchill gave me some good advice. He said, 'Keep your friends close, and your enemies even closer' so I do." Putting his arm around Maisky's shoulder and pulling him close, he said "Now Comrade, I will not shake your hand, but come and have some Polish vodka with me!"

Maisky recognised the slight and pulled away, saying "My delegation has had a long flight and little sleep. We have to leave very soon. I will convey your agreement to Comrade Stalin and the Politburo. I look forward to what co-operation we can arrange, but this meeting must remain completely secret and we have not met. Good morning Comrade General, good morning Lieutenant." and he nodded towards Sexton as he departed with his adjutant.

After the door had closed Sikorski said "My Russian is not very good. What did the adjutant say to Maisky?" Terry fumed "He said 'tell him we will carry out an investigation. Just stall him."

Sikorski spluttered "Anders is completely right. These people are barbarians, we should have no dealings with them. But my hands are tied. Without Russia the Allies have no chance of defeating Hitler, and if I refuse to lead my people, Churchill and Roosevelt will soon find someone else and I will end up in a ditch."

As Terry accompanied the General back to his room he was asked what his plans were next. "Well, I have to get back to London, and I am hoping to travel in your aircraft, but I cannot afford to be seen, so I need to get aboard after everyone else and hide in the back."

That shouldn't be a problem," said Sikorski, "I'll have a word with the pilot. Mak Prchal can be totally trusted and he can arrange it."

"Mak Prchal! I met him with you in Heliopolis. He and I will work something out, it'll be no problem."

Chapter 19
Departure and Disaster

With the Sikorski and Maisky parties safely back in their rooms, plans for the flight back to London were prepared. At about ten am the Governor and his wife returned and took coffee in the dining room with Maisky. MacFarlane and Maisky had agreed that it would not be prudent for him and General Sikorski to be seen anywhere near each other, but as the General had some duties to perform in the town before evening, Maisky had agreed to leave as soon as possible. For the benefit of his colleagues who were also ignorant of the meeting, by pre-arrangement, an airman arrived and advised Macfarlane that deteriorating weather at Cairo meant that the Maisky Liberator needed to take off at eleven am at the latest.

There was a flurry of activity as Maisky's adjutant rounded up the rest of the party and they set off for the airfield. With a sigh of relief Macfarlane told General Sikorski that his people could now roam freely around the residence. Terry Sexton however, with increasing frustration, had to stay secreted in his room.

The reason for dispatching Ivan Maisky so precipitately was that after lunch, General Sikorski was scheduled to make a tour of inspection of the excavation works that was in full swing on the Rock. A complex network of tunnels and defensive works was under way to enable Gibraltar to be defended in the event of attack by land and sea. The totally unexpected assault on the land side of Singapore had convinced Churchill that Gibraltar should be protected on all sides.

After this visit Sikorski and his party went to join a sherry reception at the American mission, held to celebrate the fourth of July. The Americans and several of the French diplomats also present were astounded to find Sikorski in their midst and an animated discussion ensued.

After about two hours Sikorski excused himself and headed back to the Convent where he had convened an informal drinks party of his officers. He had also invited the pilot Mak Prchal to the meeting and proceeded to award medals to several of his officers and to the pilot, who had flown him many times in the past.

All this time Terry Sexton had been cooped up in his room as only Sikorski, Macfarlane and Adam Kulakowski knew of his presence on the Rock, all of whom had been with the touring party. Terry had not eaten since breakfast. However he had consoled himself with a bottle of Veterano. At last Kulakowski arrived with a tray of hot food, together with Mak Prchal.

They greeted each other as old friends and planned how they would get Terry onto the Liberator. Take off was scheduled for eleven pm so it would be dark. Terry would travel in the car with Sikorski, Macfarlane and Kulakowski, ensuring that no questions were asked by the security guards on the airfield. The car would make a tour of the airfield, and Terry would be dropped off at the western end of the runway. He would then lay low until the aircraft was due to take off, which, as the wind was easterly, would start in the west.

"What is the best way for me to board?" he asked. Will someone open the rear hatch?"

"No," said Prchal, "that would attract too much attention from the passengers. Whilst I am running up the engines for take-off checks, you can climb up through the nosewheel bay. It is very tight, but the maintenance crews do it all the time. It brings you up into the bomb-aimers position, but as this is not used we use it to store baggage. You can squeeze up from there into the cockpit and use the jump seat. Jockey will help you up and the curtain will make sure no-one sees you."

At about ten thirty pm General Sikorski's party climbed into three cars and headed towards the airfield. Sikorski with MacFarlane went in the last car, Sikorski in front next to the driver. The car was driven to the west end of the Convent where Adam Kulakowski and Terry Sexton were concealed behind a side door. As the car drew level they swiftly entered the rear of the car and Terry settled down low between MacFarlane and Kulakowski.

When they arrived at the airfield, Macfarlane sat upright in the front seat and rolled down his window. They had caught up the other two cars so the barrier was open. The Governor gave a casual wave to the guard who scarcely had time to see into the car before they drove onto the base. Just past the guardhouse their car turned sharply right and headed for the western edge of the airfield. Every three hundred yards or so a guard was standing on watch, or patrolling up and down the water's edge. When the car got to about two hundred yards from the end of the runway, it slowed down and stopped next to a guard who sprang to attention.

"I'll get out and distract him," said Macfarlane. "If you come with me General, you can inspect him whilst the car turns around on the runway and Lieutenant Sexton gets out."

Macfarlane and Sikorski got out of the car and went up to the guard. Macfarlane turned to the car and shouted "Go and turn around on the runway and come back for us."

Sikorski inspected the guard who stood stiffly to attention, with his back to the car as it drove off. "Very smart, soldier," said Sikorski, "you are a credit to your Unit. What Unit is that?"

"Number twenty-seven ADRU Sir!" Shouted the airman. "Well airman, "said Macfarlane, "stand at ease. This is General Sikorski, Prime Minister of the Polish Government, and you are very privileged to meet him. "Yes sir! A pleasure Sir!" responded the guard, snapping to a very uneasy-looking 'at ease' position.

Whilst all this was going on the car had sped to the end of the runway and Terry Sexton had rolled out onto the edge of the tarmac and concealed himself in a clump of grassy rocks. It reminded him of another time, many years earlier it seemed, when he had hidden in the same uncomfortable place.

The car returned to where the small group was standing and as they said farewell to the guard, Kulakowski got out and opened the doors for the two Generals. They boarded and the car set off towards the airfield office buildings.

Terry spent a very uncomfortable half hour cramped up between the rocks near the water's edge, keeping out of view of the patrolling airmen. After what seemed an age, he heard the sound of engines starting up, and then saw the Liberator lumbering towards him as it back-tracked the runway. When it reached the end of the runway it slowly turned on the circular pad.

Once it had lined up with the runway, the pilot started to check the engines, running each one up to full speed for several minutes. The backwash from the propellers blew into Terry's eyes as he raised his head to see where the guards were.

To his consternation he saw that two of the guards had met at the end of their beats and were smoking, watching the aircraft. If he had not seen the glow of their cigarettes he would have left his hiding place and been seen. The aircraft finished running up the engines and sat on the tarmac throbbing noisily. The pilot then started to do the full and free control movement checks and Terry could see the elevators and rudder flipping up and down and from side to side.

The guards seemed to be waiting for the Liberator to take off. After about fifteen minutes, with their cigarettes finished, they resumed their patrolling. Once they were well on their way, Terry climbed out of the rocks and scuttled across to the aircraft. He knew that he only had two or three minutes before the guards returned. Carefully avoiding the whirring propellers he crawled underneath the nose of the Liberator.

The belly of the aircraft was very close to the ground but the open nosewheel doors gave just enough room for him to squeeze inside. He clambered up onto the undercarriage struts and found a small access hole into the nose of the aircraft. It was very cramped and full of mailbags. In forcing himself in, he dislodged one of the mailbags which fell halfway down into the undercarriage bay. As he reached for it he heard the voice of Squadron Leader Haydock, the co-pilot.

"What's wrong? What took you so long?"

"Too many guards," said Terry. "Now I've dropped a mailbag."

"Leave it," said Haydock. "We have to go."

"Its stuck, I can't lift it. I'll just have to push it right out."

"That's ok, they'll pick it up and send it on tomorrow. Just come inside."

Terry kicked at the mailbag and it fell onto the runway. He wriggled around and Haydock helped pull him into the cockpit. Haydock handed him a lifejacket and got back into his seat. Prchal said "What was the delay, we nearly set off without you?" Terry explained about the guards and Prchal said "put on your life jacket and lower the jump seat. It only has a lap belt but it's good enough."

"I can't stand these fiddly jackets" Terry commented, but he put it on anyway. "Besides, you're not wearing yours." Prchal's jacket was hooked over the back of his seat.

Prchal joked "It's bad luck to wear a life jacket!" and Terry riposted "It's damn bad luck not to wear one!"

When he was safely strapped into his seat they prepared for take-off. Jockey Haydock asked Prchal's permission to do the take-off, saying "I've only done two night take-offs, both from the left seat. I'd like to do one from the co-pilot's seat."

"Not this time I'm afraid," said Prchal, "it's too late for a full briefing and the horizon is only just visible. Besides, we've got important cargo. You just do the gear and flaps."

Prchal repeated the full and free checks of ailerons, elevators and rudder, and called for half flap. Haydock operated the flap lever and checked the flap position indicator. "Half flap" he called.

Terry watched with interest as Prchal opened up the throttles, slowly at first and then to the full open position. As the speed built up Haydock called it out until "165 knots – rotate!" and Prchal pulled back on the control yoke. Once the aircraft was climbing Haydock called "Wheel brakes – gear up!" The wheel brakes were small pedals on the side of the rudder pedals in both pilot and co-pilot positions and as Haydock stabbed at them the aircraft began to turn to the left and Prchal started to correct it saying "I have control!"

When the rumbling of the wheels stopped, Haydock reached for the parking brake lever and then operated the landing gear handle. The parking brake lever on the central control console falls naturally under the right hand of the pilot sitting in the left-hand seat and a co-pilot has to reach over the console to operate it. However the control lock lever falls naturally under the left hand of the co-pilot in a mirrored position and Haydock had unconsciously operated this instead of the parking brake.

Normally the control lock would not engage unless the elevator and rudder controls were in exactly the neutral positions, but as the aircraft reached about 150 feet in altitude Prchal eased the control yoke forward so as to gain speed. At the same time he was operating the rudder to correct the swing to the left. As a result, unknown to him, the control lock pins slid into place as the rudder and elevator control rods passed through their neutral positions.

A few seconds later when Prchal came to pull back into the climb he realised that the controls were locked. He immediately rolled back the elevator trim wheel to climb but to his surprise it put the aircraft into a slight descent. "Check the control lock!" he shouted to Haydock, who immediately realised his error and reached for the control lock. It was stiff as Prchal was pulling the controls against the locking pins but the lock eventually came free.

The Liberator started to level off but it was too late. "Cut mags!" shouted Prchal, at the same time cutting the throttles. Haydock flipped the ignition switches just as the aircraft hit the water. The half-retracted undercarriage struck first and lurched the aircraft forward onto its nose, and it somersaulted upside down and smashed onto the surface of the Mediterranean.

Terry, who had seen the accident unfold, came to a few seconds later feeling as though he had been kicked in the stomach. He was hanging upside down in his seat harness and was disorientated for a while until he got his bearings. The cockpit was slowly filling with water from the smashed-in windscreen. Prchal was hanging upside down in his seat and Haydock was nowhere to be seen.

With great difficulty owing to his weight pulling against it, Terry was able to undo his harness and he fell onto the inverted roof of the aircraft. Above him he could see Prchal with a deep cut on his face where it had hit the control wheel. He was clearly dazed and disorientated but Terry was able to reach up and undo his seat harness, catching him as he fell. Prchal's life jacket had fallen off the back of his seat and Terry was able to help him put it on and do up most of the straps.

The aircraft was now rapidly filling with water so Terry pushed Prchal out through the smashed windscreen and followed him out. On the surface He could see very little, just the lights at the end of the runway. Of Prchal, Haydock or any other survivors he could see nothing, so he set off swimming towards the lights.

Reaching land, Terry heard the sound of a motor boat heading out towards the scene of the crash. He realised that he was in a very tricky situation. His presence on the aircraft, if it became known was likely to cause acute embarrassment to the UK Government and to the Allies generally, so he resolved to keep a low profile and try to get back to the Governor's house.

Chapter 20
Aftermath

A tired and shaken Lieutenant-General Mason-Macfarlane unlocked his study door and entered. He was amazed to see a very bedraggled Terry Sexton squatting on the floor almost naked, drying out his clothes in front of the electric fire. "What happened? How did you get in?" asked a bemused Macfarlane.

"Your security guards had other distractions" said Terry, then asked about the other passengers. "Only the pilot survived," said Macfarlane. "He's in hospital but can't recall anything. One of the passengers was still alive when we got to him but he died by the time we got him to land. How did you get out?"

Terry briefly explained what had happened to the Liberator and how Haydock had inadvertently locked the controls. He asked about General Sikorski and his daughter. "Sikorski is dead and Madame Lesniowska is missing, we must assume she is dead. This is a dreadful disaster. The ramifications for relations with Poland and the Allies is beyond belief. There will have to be an inquiry and you will have to tell what happened. An error by a most trusted British pilot will go down very badly all round. There will be conspiracy allegations and all sorts of complications. Maisky's Liberator was parked right next to Sikorski's for god's sake! The Poles will have a field day on this!"

Despite his wet clothes and shaking body Terry tried to be a calming influence. "Don't do or say anything precipitate.

Leave it to London to decide how to act. For god's sake don't tell anyone about my presence. If there's to be an investigation it will take time to set up. I need to get back to London as soon as possible and find out how they want it handled. Can you arrange that with Group Captain Bolland?"

"Yes I'm sure that can be arranged. Meanwhile I'll file a report to the Foreign Office giving brief details."

"I suggest you do no such thing. We're not sure if the Germans have broken some of our codes and if they get hold of this it will be dynamite. This information can only go by courier. I can do it, or you can send someone on the same aircraft, but best not to use W/T."

"Perhaps you're right. I have more pressing problems anyway. The papers in the wreck. I have boats guarding it overnight. I don't want Spanish or Italian frogmen searching it. Buster Crab and his crew are going down at first light to try and retrieve Sikorski's briefcase and any other papers. God, it would be a disaster if they washed up on a Spanish beach, with all the Polish government papers, and any references to the Maisky meeting. I only hope they haven't already floated free!"

"Actually," added Macfarlane, "it gives me an idea for a deception plan that maybe we could use in the future. A plane crash, followed by Top Secret papers washing up on enemy shores. Could come in useful sometime!"

At eleven o'clock that morning a freshly washed and dressed Terry Sexton climbed on board an RAF Transport Command Avro York and set off for the UK. Landing at

Lyneham late that night a waiting car carried him swiftly to Sir Cedric Attenby's house in Eastcote where he arrived at about one in the morning.

Sir Cedric listened with increasing disbelief as Terry unfolded the story of the events of the past two days, excluding the Maisky meeting. Within a few minutes Sir Cedric had arranged a meeting with the Anthony Eden the Foreign Minister for eight that morning and then Terry was able to get a few hours sleep.

In his Westminster office, the Minister had heard only a minute or two of Terry's tale when he excused himself and left the room. He returned very quickly and said "You better come with me. The Prime Minister wants to see us."

A short walk took the three of them to the entrance to the underground Cabinet Rooms where Winston Churchill spent much of his time. Descending several flights of stairs and passing many armed guards, all of whom, despite his well known public profile, checked the Minister's identification documents, they eventually came to the Prime Minister's inner sanctum.

Winston Churchill sat in a low armchair wearing a drab siren suit that fitted snugly around his portly waist. "Now then Anthony, who have we here?" The Minister introduced Terry and explained that he was an agent of the SOE but on special operations on behalf of Poland. Terry recounted for yet a third time the events at Gibraltar, only this time he had to include the Maisky meeting, whilst the Prime Minister listened attentively. After a few moments thought, Churchill said "You were never there, you saw and heard nothing. There is bound to be an Inquiry. Whatever comes out will not involve our diplomatic or intelligence services. No Inquiry will blame a dead British officer, no matter what the pilot says. It will be unexplained. I will instruct the necessary people. Thank you Lieutenant Sexton for your concise explanation. It will not go unnoticed." With a brief wave of his cigar the Prime Minister dismissed Terry from his presence and signalled Sir Cedric to stay.

Half an hour later Sir Cedric arrived back at his Baker Street office where Terry was waiting for him. They reviewed the situation. "Seems to me Clam that we had best carry on as if nothing happened in Gibraltar. Let the brass hats sort it out. As long as you keep your mouth shut and get on with the important work, it will eventually blow over. Where are you off to next?"

"Back to Warsaw," said Terry. "Our agent Limpet in the Abwehr communications office for Army Group 1 is making some progress. The Polish traffic analysis on the German Order of Battle in Russia is giving good intelligence but our problem is getting it to the Russians without giving away our sources. He is doing good work by making coding errors so that the Russians can try to crack some of the messages."

Sir Cedric then announced "Don't make it too easy for them. Now Clam, it is time to brief you on a top secret matter. There are only a very small number of people who know about this. The PM has just authorised me to add you to the list. So far the Abwehr is putting the leaks down to interpretation of radio traffic patterns. However, the fact is, we have cracked Enigma. For several years now we have been collating intelligence information called Boniface that is classified Ultra Top Secret. In fact Winston has renamed it ULTRA. The coded messages you have been sending back to us have been read and we are using them to drip-feed information to the Russians. They don't know we have cracked it and it is essential that they don't know. The PM is thinking strategically. After the war we don't know who our friends or enemies will be. Any edge we can have on intelligence will be invaluable."

Terry said that he was not surprised and had guessed as much. Otherwise, why was London so emphatic in wanting the coded German messages forwarded from Eastern Europe?

Sir Cedric emphasised the need for caution. "It's invaluable having the Poles making those intercepts as our own listeners can't get adequate reception of what's going on at the Russian front, but if the Germans get the slightest wind that we are cracking Enigma, that we are feeding ULTRA information to our field commanders, they will change everything. They have already changed rotor numbers and coding procedures. Each time it takes us weeks to get back on track."

"So why are you telling me all this?" asked Terry "If it is so hush-hush why risk sending me back with this knowledge?"

"Because we need someone out there who appreciates the whole picture. Opportunities may arise which you can recognise and exploit which may otherwise go un-noticed. The downside is that if you are caught you will have to swallow the pill straight away. You don't want to be caught out again. The Germans are already suspecting we have cracked the code."

Terry said "Don't worry, I'll bite the bullet. I know that Doenitz in the German Admiralty has already instigated at least two reviews of Enigma because of his growing U-boat losses. So far they have concluded that any intelligence gained is due to traffic patterns or agents. They have had two purges of cipher clerks but so far Limpet is in the clear. Their absolutely logical minds are convinced that Enigma cannot be broken because of the huge number of coding combinations."

"Let's keep it that way, we don't want Limpet getting caught."

Terry spent the next two days with Vivien at their little house in Amersham and he was amazed to see how little Sarah had grown. With a sad heart he took his leave again and travelled to the base at Tempsford in Bedfordshire.

On 9th July 1943, as dusk started to fall, he took off in a specially modified American Hudson bomber for the trip to Warsaw. An additional fuel tank had been fitted into the fuselage to give it the required range to get to Warsaw, but the aircraft would have to be re-fuelled on the ground. This was an extremely dangerous activity, not only because of the time it took but also because the stolen fuel tanker had to be hidden after to the landing as enemy search parties would be trying to locate it.

Night started to fall as the aircraft made its way over the North Sea, routing north-east towards Denmark. As it approached the Danish coast darkness fell rapidly and the pilot took the aircraft down to about six hundred feet to avoid radar. The Hudson skimmed along the coast of Poland until it reached Danzig then turned inland and headed direct for Warsaw. As they approached Plonsk Terry prepared for the landing. The pilot soon announced that they were over Kampinoski Park and climbed the Hudson to one thousand feet and started circling. Suddenly a lamp flashed the Morse code letter 'M' for Mike from the ground. The pilot immediately flashed back his own code letter 'A' for Apple, and three lights appeared in the park, forming a letter 'L'.

The pilot slowed the aircraft and made a steady approach to the triangle of lights. Aligning with the long side of the 'L' the pilot slowed down to just above stalling speed as the Hudson touched down and after a short run came to a stop. The pilot immediately turned the aircraft through a half-turn and taxied back to the start of the primitive grass runway in the rough field. Turning once more into wind, he lined up for a quick take-off if danger threatened.

Terry quickly exited the bomb bay, whilst a group of partisans started to re-fuel the aircraft. It took twelve agonising minutes to complete the task then the aircraft started its departure run. It took over three hundred and fifty yards before it crept into the air and climbed away. The oil-burning lights at the edges of the field were quickly extinguished as the flak started again. With a sense of relief Terry heard the Hudson swoop north and head off into the distance as the ack-ack fire gradually died away.

Whilst he collected his black bag of equipment, a pair of black-clad figures came towards him. He was immensely relieved to recognise Drolonski and Zcezeski who bundled him towards a motor-cycle combination at the side of a narrow road. Both were unusually silent and grim faced. Terry rode in the sidecar and within ten minutes they were in the safe house on the outskirts of Warsaw.

Terry warmed his hands in front of a wood stove and the two agents flanked him. Terry sensed a hovering menace. Drolonski, Agent Barnacle, spat out gruffly "you know the latest Clam? General Sikorski has been murdered by you British in a plane crash!"

Terry had to restrain himself but replied "I heard about it, but it was an accident!"

"No, it was no accident! It has been on the news direct from Berlin! The British and Russians arranged it. He was assassinated to weaken our government! He was an embarrassment to the Allies."

"No, that is just what the Germans want you to believe, to destroy our co-operation. Don't you see!" retorted Terry. "General Sikorski was our greatest friend in occupied Europe, we needed him. His death is a tragedy; it is the last thing we wanted."

The two agents took a lot of convincing, but Terry could not tell them all he knew about the accident. However deep down they knew he was right and their attitude gradually relaxed.

Chapter 21
Rescue

Terry asked "What's the latest here? Have we had any success?"

Zcezeski, code name Shrimp, said "Yes, we have been able to derail some arms trains, but at a heavy cost. The Gestapo are making reprisal attacks on the villages and many men have been shot. Prawn and Krill have been sent to Pawiak prison and have been taken a couple of times to Szucha Avenue interrogation centre in the middle of Warsaw to be questioned. I fear they may crack so I have disbanded their circuits and relocated the agents to other circuits. We have been planning a rescue attempt for their next transfer, otherwise we may just have to eliminate them."

Terry responded "I don't think rescue is a good idea, it will only cause more reprisals. We may get away with elimination, and it is less risky. When is it due?"

We don't know. We just have to keep a sharp watch but there are many prisoners coming and going to Szucha Avenue. We do have an agent, Whelk, in the prison who can signal when it's them on their way in the truck. We can't use radio or landlines so we just have a man in the street who signals us. The journey takes about half an hour but we can lay on an ambush within ten minutes."

"Then let's do it. From what we know about number twenty-five Szucha, we will be doing them a favour. What else is going on in the Sector?"

Prawn replied "A number of kids have got arrested and taken to the prison. They too have been backwards and forwards to Szucha. Mere Kids! Tortured to within an inch of their lives! The Gestapo are just animals!"

"Can we do anything about them?" asked Terry.

"No, there are too many of them. Besides they know nothing, they are not agents or part of any circuit."

The watch on the prison continued for several days but whilst several trucks emerged each day taking prisoners to various destinations, there was no signal to indicate that agents Prawn or Krill were in any of them.

After four days a boy was brought into the safe house by Barnacle. He had been released from the interrogation centre on Szucha Avenue because of his youth. Julian Kulski was only sixteen years old but looked much younger. He had helped the Polish resistance at low level by acting as a lookout. Kept in Pawiak prison, he had been taken to Szucha several times for interrogation, but not tortured. His questioners had been rough and bullying, but having got nowhere, decided to release him and follow him.

Kulski had readily given his shadow the slip but dared not go home so he had contacted the resistance and been taken to Barnacle. He was very shaken and sobbing as he told of the conditions inside the Szucha centre. He had heard intolerable screams and shouts and the sounds of vicious beatings. On the morning of his release he had been taken to a small room.

"There were three girls taken there from prison with me," he said. They had been in the Underground Army and captured in a raid and sentenced to death. "The Gestapo stripped them, and raped them in front of me, using bottles and knives."

He broke down again into sobs. "One of them, Barbara, died. The other two are back at the prison but are being taken out tomorrow and shot."

Terry looked at Barnacle and Shrimp and said in a steely voice, "We have to do something about this. Where will they take them?"

Barnacle thought slowly and said "Usually they execute them in a field about two miles from Kampinoski Park. They have an area that they use as an execution yard and for mass graves. Are you thinking the same as me? Can we intercept them?"

"Again, we risk reprisals. But we can't knowingly let this happen. We just have to show the Polish people that we care and can act." said Terry vehemently. "Can Whelk in Pawiak tell us when they are leaving?"

"Yes, but when they take people for execution, they go in an open-top truck so all the population can see them, as a deterrent. They usually leave about half past eight when there are lots of people about. We just need to have a watcher outside. It's not easy as the other end as the Park itself is a closed zone to Poles. We know which direction they are heading so we can lay an ambush. They usually have a lead car and one behind, both full of troops so we need to plan it carefully. We can lay roadside charges triggered by men with long wires. Leave it to me!" said Shrimp.

The next morning four open-topped trucks swept out of the heavy gates leading to the courtyard inside Pawiak Prison. The first truck contained armed troops and in the second truck were five women, handcuffed and standing upright with four guards around them. Two of the women were identified as the young girls Kulski had seen. The third truck contained four male prisoners similarly guarded whilst the last truck again was full of troops.

The trucks turned north along the walls of the prison and then westwards towards the outskirts of Warsaw. Lookouts had been positioned at each end of the fortress in case the convoy went a different way, but the message was quickly passed to .the ambush party by short wave radio. A crude code was used and the message was kept short, but the indication was that there were more trucks than had been planned for.

The ambush site had been chosen in a wooded area near Kampinoski Park, on a sharp left-hand bend in the road. The intention was to bunch up the convoy. Charges had been laid on both sides of the road in the verges, in two locations three truck-lengths apart. When Terry got the message he cursed and ran out from his hiding place in the trees with Shrimp. They scooped up the rear pair of charges and paced back seven paces and replaced them in the grass verge. They then had to carefully re-lay the wires that ran back into the woods where other agents lay in wait to ignite the charges.

Running back into the woods Clam quickly briefed the waiting resistance members about the changes in circumstances. In particular he was concerned about the guards in the prisoners' trucks.

Interminable minutes passed and then an agent further up the road towards Warsaw waved a yellow flag and dived into the forest. Soon the four trucks came into sight travelling at high speed. They slowed to negotiate the corner and at the same time a cyclist pushed his bike out of the woods into the path of the leading truck, which slowed to walking pace. The cyclist suddenly dropped his bike and dived into the woods. A second later the first two charges on either side of the front truck exploded into a mass of flame and the truck leapt into the air and crashed back upside down.

A moment later as the last truck drew level with the rear charges, they too exploded and the truck disintegrated. Those in the middle two trucks were completely dazed and disorientated by the explosions and the guards were quickly overcome by the partisans who rushed out of the woods. The prisoners were taken into the woods and after the guards had been relieved of their keys, the handcuffs were removed and put on the surviving guards.

The agents were at a loss at first because of the unexpectedly large number of freed prisoners. Then Terry was struck with an idea. "Well lay a false trail. Barnacle, you take the party back through the woods and disperse the freed prisoners between the safe houses. Shrimp, you come with me and we'll drive the trucks away beyond the Park in the opposite direction and abandon them. We'll have to make our own way back, but we're used to that."

"Don't worry Clam," interposed Barnacle, I'll come back with the motor-cycle combo and collect you. The others can take the partisans to the safe houses."

When Terry returned to his safe house the two condemned girls Irena and Krystyna were there with Barnacle and Kulski and a doctor. Their gratitude knew no bounds but they were in a pitiful state and would need several weeks to recover from their ordeal.

Eight guards had been killed in the leading and trailing trucks when the roadside charges had been detonated, but Terry had hoped that by leaving the guards from the other two trucks unharmed, that there would be no reprisals. He was wrong, and the next morning ten men were seized at random off the streets of Warsaw and taken to Pawiak. They were loaded into heavily armed trucks and sent to the execution field. The agent in the prison signalled that the two agents in Pawiak were also being sent for execution. The trucks were accompanied by five armoured cars. There was simply no time for the partisans to arrange a rescue ambush and if they had they would have faced overwhelming odds.

Later that day news came through that the executions had been carried out. Despite the fury in the partisans' camp, Terry was secretly relieved that in their haste to seek retribution, the SS had not been able to extract any information from Prawn and Krill.

For three months the partisans carried out acts of sabotage on railways and bridges to hinder in any way they could the German transport to the Eastern Front. They also made long term plans for when and if the tide turned and the Wehrmacht went into retreat from the Russian armies which were growing in strength.

In late November 1943 Terry was recalled to London once more for substantive discussions on the situation with other agencies and the British and Polish governments. The Polish Prime Minister in Exile Stanislaw Mikolajczyk was increasingly concerned at the barbaric reprisals being heaped upon the general populace in Poland after each sabotage raid. He feared a total loss of public confidence and support and wanted to scale down the operations until later in the course of the war.

Despite the Russians being allies, they were making it clear that they intended to hold on to any Polish territory that they regained. Mikolajczyk wanted the Interallié to replace some of the direct action with a propaganda programme to persuade the population to agitate for democratic elections in the future. This was agreed as a strategy and Terry set to work with Sir Cedric at Baker Street to produce a plan of action.

Making his way home to Amersham that evening, Terry felt a pang of apprehension. It was nothing concrete, just a vague feeling of unease. He let himself into the house and Sarah ran up to meet him. As he hoisted her into his arms he saw Vivien coming out of the kitchen with a huge smile on her face He immediately saw why. She was clearly very pregnant again. His face lighted up as she came to embrace him.

Terry put Sarah down and she scampered off into the dining room.

Terry was exuberant. They spent the time after supper playing with Sarah until she went to bed, then they sat together in comfortable intimacy for the rest of the evening.

Sir Cedric was waiting for him when he arrived at the offices next morning. Your Hudson from Tempsford will be ready this evening and we are sending your stores on ahead, but I've been asked to send you to Portland Place to see the Poles. They wouldn't say what for, but no doubt they have messages for you to take."

His taxi dropped him off at the door to the Government in Exile's offices and he walked the gauntlet of heavy security to get to the reception area. He was immediately taken by an equerry to the third floor and to the anteroom to the Prime Minister's office, where a secretary gave him a sealed folder of papers to take back to Poland. Within seconds Stanislaw Mikolajczyk came out to meet him and invited him in to his room. He spoke briefly about their meeting the previous day, then they were joined by General Kazimierz Sonkowski the Commander-in Chief of Polish forces.

In a short ceremony the Prime Minister awarded Terry the Order of Polonia Restituta, the highest award made to a civilian for work towards securing the freedom of Poland.

Chapter 22
Limpet

The battle of Kursk raged on during July and August 1943 but the Russians were well prepared for it. Some of the information that Limpet had provided back to London enabled much of the Nazi plans to be read and the intelligence service was able to skilfully feed this back without letting the Russians know the source.

Part of Limpet's job in the Nazi communications centre was to pass to each Wehrmacht army group the settings for the Enigma machines. Initially these were changed every week but just prior to the battle they were changed to daily settings. Doenitz had insisted that security be tightened for all Enigma users. Although he had been assured that the code had not been broken, he was taking no chances.

The security was very tight. Limpet was put on a twelve hour shift. He started at fifteen minutes to midnight and had to telephone out the settings to his twenty-five stations before five minutes to the hour. He then had to stay on shift until fifteen minutes to mid-day, thus ensuring that he could not see the settings to be used for the rest of the day. It also meant that any morning settings were out of date by the time he went off duty.

Despite this all the operators in his office were searched thoroughly when they went off duty. This was of no consequence to Limpet, as he had memorised the settings. It was not difficult because there were only six rotor wheel settings and ten plugboard settings. By the time he had repeated them to his opposite numbers in each of the army group communications centres, they were imprinted on his memory, so when he got back to his home he could encipher them and wireless them back to England.

The rest of his shift consisted of taking messages and encoding them on an Enigma machine. Most of these were administrative information, or about minor tactical Wehrmacht deployments. Some of them however were of more strategic importance and he succeeded in sending some of this back to London.

The defeat of the Wehrmacht at Kursk in the middle of August was the start of an inexorable advance by the Russians back across their own country, and then into Poland. Limpet's office was relocated to Cracow and then to Posnan and he rented a small two bedroom flat and moved his mother in with him. As the winter of 1943 turned into a bitter spring of 1944 his intelligence continued to inform London of the dispositions of German divisions, which in turn was used to discreetly advise the Russian troops.

All during this time the Interallié partisans continued to harass the retreating Wehrmacht troops with acts of sabotage, demolition and cutting of communications. The Germans in turn responded with harsh reprisals and repression, sending many Polish citizens to labour camps and extermination camps. Rebellion was seething in the Polish partisans camps and as the Russians approached plans were being made for an uprising in Warsaw. The memory of the brutal destruction of the ghetto was still very raw. Pleas were sent out for the Russians to converge on Warsaw when the uprising took place.

In June came the heartening news of the Normandy invasion in which the French resistance networks had played such a vital part. Terry was still in contact with Thrush and learnt about the messages which had been sent in clear over the BBC. Extracts of poems were used to trigger sabotage acts behind the German lines, disrupting rail networks and communications. This had helped to delay for valuable hours the Nazi counter attacks.

The Allies were also making inroads into the Italian peninsula and at the beginning of September the Italians asked for an armistice.. The Germans immediately retaliated and reinforced their forces in Northern Italy so Terry was recalled once again.

"The Gestapo are on a killing spree in Italy," said Sir Cedric. "Not only the Italian army, but the whole of the partisan network is dispirited and demoralised." A hundred civilians are being killed for every German killed by partisans, and ten for every German wounded. It can't go on. Macfarlane has asked for you. We need to rebuild the network and resume sabotage. Progress of the Allies in the mountains is far slower than planned and we need to weaken the Germans supply lines. He wants you sent to Italy to help organise the British element of the resistance."

Terry's journey on this occasion was relatively straightforward as he flew from Gibraltar direct to the airbase at Brindisi which had just been captured. He very quickly co-ordinated networks of agents to lead the partisans and to harass the Wehrmacht which was putting up a stubborn resistance in the central Apennine Mountains.

Chapter 23
Uprising

At the end of July the Polish uprising began and vicious fighting took place in the streets of Warsaw. However the Russian army remained resolutely in its place a few miles to the east of the city having been brought to a halt by General Model's Army Group North and the Russians made no attempt to relieve the siege. The western Allies considered what they could do to help the city and decided to divert aircraft from the bombing of the Ploesti oilfields to send relief flights to Warsaw.

The Mediterranean Allied Air Force was based at Brindisi with Squadron 178 consisting of Liberators and commenced relief flights on the fourth of August. It suffered severe casualties from fighter aircraft based at Szombathely airfield in Hungary which was on the direct route to Warsaw. On the seventh of August Liberators of 178 Squadron attacked the airfield but suffered heavy casualties from anti-aircraft fire. Relief flights resumed a week later and continued until mid September but the efforts were in vain. Eventually the resistance leaders in Warsaw capitulated and large numbers of Poles were systematically executed by the Wehrmacht.

The uprising had been planned by the resistance to try and take control of Warsaw before the city was overrun by the Russians, in an attempt to secure the basis of a post-war Polish state but the failure of the resistance led to the Russians rapidly invading the rest of Poland.

In Italy the fight for liberation was long drawn out with fierce German resistance in the hills and mountains of the centre of the country. Clam's partisans played their part in disrupting enemy supplies and after the capture and execution of Mussolini, Terry was recalled and sent once more to Poland, this time to work behind Russian lines.

His instructions this time were for a new strategy. Instead of working behind the German lines to cause disruption, the objective now was to slow the Russian advance into Germany. Churchill's belief was that 'possession is nine-tenths of the law' and he and Roosevelt wanted the Western Front to advance as far as possible into Germany before the Russians got there. They particularly wanted to occupy Berlin.

Organising sabotage and intelligence networks behind the Russian lines was an extremely difficult task for Terry as the population was disrupted by the massive destruction left by the retreating Nazis and by the outright rape and pillage exacted by the advancing Russians. Thousands of Polish citizens were shipped off to Gulags in Russia and cruel retribution was dealt to the population after sabotage attacks. His circuits were frequently broken by the disappearance of his agents. Obtaining explosives and ammunition was becoming impossible.

The chaos had one advantage and that was that freedom of movement was less restricted. None of the population had identity papers and the invading army were too preoccupied with looting to stop and question everyone. By November the disruption to the network was such that Terry decided to disband it and try to get back behind the German lines to make contact with the resistance movement there in preparation for the final collapse of the Reich. He was determined to find out what Limpet had been able to do.

With the Russian advance Limpet's Wermacht communications headquarters was relocated to Berlin. This time it was more difficult for him to take his mother with him because of her Polish birth. but he argued strongly that her husband had been a true German and Nazi and she had her pension to prove it. After a long battle in which he pointed out how bad it would be if a Nazi war widow were captured by the Russians, she was allowed to join him.

Several people in his office had declined to move and as a result he was promoted to head of the section. This meant that he had access to more information, but was more closely monitored by the SS officers based in the building. He was able to see the Enigma machine settings well in advance of their use and, at great peril, was able occasionally to send them back to London. This was as well because as a result of Admiral Doenitz' suspicions about Enigma, the setting changes were now every six hours and it was even more difficult to get the rapidly changing information out.

Terry's disguise was as a wounded crew member of a Panzer which had been set on fire by a Russian T34 tank in the battle for Kursk. He took the name of the tank driver Kurt Pfeiffer whose body tags had been recovered and who had been buried in an unmarked mass grave. Pfeiffer's papers had been destroyed in the fire and the new hastily forged papers would not stand close scrutiny. However in the chaos after the battle there were many refugees and wounded German soldiers returning to Germany so he was able to get transport with a group of other troops suffering burns. He was worried that the scars from his reconstruction surgery and the fact that his wounds had healed so well might arouse suspicion from the doctors but there were many soldiers far more seriously wounded than himself and he barely received any scrutiny.

With his papers he was able to make his way to Berlin and find the apartment where Limpet lived with his mother. They were only too happy to take Terry in and he was able to re-establish contact with the German network of circuits.

At the end of October Limpet was heavily interrogated by two SS officers who questioned him closely about his family and his background. They were particularly concerned when they discovered that his in-laws had been sent from Poland to work in Germany. He feigned not to know that it was a labour camp and said that he was pleased that they had been found work at a time when there was great hardship elsewhere. After a thorough grilling the officers left and he was allowed to return to work. He was totally surprised then a week later when his mother's parents and her sister were driven up to his apartment block and released. He realised that the SS officers must have believed him and thought that for someone doing such important work, his family should be spared.

Then in the middle of November, Limpet received instructions which were very disturbing.

Chapter 24
Doenitz and Eisenhower

The room fell silent as the door was flung open and Admiral Karl Doenitz and General Walther Model entered. The two intelligence officers leapt to their feet and saluted but Doenitz waved them to sit down.

Doenitz was Grand Admiral of the Naval Fleet, having been promoted from Admiral in charge of the U-boat fleet eighteen months earlier. He was probably the brightest of the Nazi leadership and his antennae were very sharp. Whilst it had been promulgated by the Allies that Operation Overlord, the D-Day landings had taken German defences by complete surprise, Doenitz had suspected that Normandy would be the target and had sent patrol boats out into the waters off the coast at great risk, as the Allied air forces had complete mastery of the skies and carried out continuous patrols. Knowing the seas and tides as he did, the Admiral predicted just when any landing would have to take place and sent his patrols out under cover of darkness.

Just after midnight on the sixth of June a patrol boat had spotted a fleet of craft heading for Normandy. Doenitz had been informed, advised Berlin, and readied his forces.

At about four in the morning a remote listening station in Yorkshire picked up an unusual coded message. Jean Moreton had been on duty since midnight and the airwaves had been very quiet. Suddenly there was activity on the frequency that she was monitoring, which was known to emanate from the area around Calais. She quickly jotted down the coded letters on her pad and held up her hand. Her supervisor took the page from her and telephoned for a courier who drove straight to Bletchley Park with it.

Within an hour the message had been decoded and read:-

'We are thankful for our faithful comrades, they play their parts in great trouble. Heil the Fuhrer, long live Germany. Your Naval Chief.'

In the Supreme Headquarters of the Allied Expeditionary Force, SHAEF, General Dwight D Eisenhower was disconcerted by the message. The landings in Normandy were in full swing, but if Doenitz had alerted Berlin as early as two in the morning, a full counter attack could be expected at any minute. It was only much later that the Allies learnt that the message from Doenitz had been disregarded, as the Chiefs of Staff were convinced by Hitler that the invasion would come along the Calais coast. In addition, Hitler himself had slept undisturbed until well into the morning before he had been advised that the invasion had begun.

Now, in this anteroom in Berlin, Doenitz was following another of his hunches. When his meeting with the Fuhrer ended, he asked Rear Admiral Otto Schulz, head of Naval Intelligence, and General Albert Praun, Chief Signals Officer of Army Group Centre to join himself and Model to discuss signals security.

Doenitz began, "Gentlemen, thank you for waiting so long. The Fuhrer had much to discuss but now we can join you.

General Model and I have agreed that the situation requires inter-service co-operation and you are best placed to advise.

The situation as we see it is that there is a strong possibility that the Allies are breaking some of our Enigma codes. We know that the Poles broke some messages before the war, but we have increased our rotor and plugboard combinations by a factor of many millions. The question is, would it still be possible to break it?"

Praun responded to the question with another question. "What makes you think the codes may be being read?"

Doenitz explained "For two years now we have been experiencing an increasing rate of U-boat losses. Whenever a vessel surfaces to re-provision from our mother ships, or to attack a convoy, there are nearly always destroyers waiting. I don't think it can be a coincidence."

"I don't agree" interjected Schulz. "The Atlantic is thick with Allied convoys and each one is surrounded by destroyers. It is even becoming more difficult for the U-boats to find a clear enough space to rendezvous the mother ships. Anyway, the Allies have mobile direction finders on their ships and can home in on our U-boats when they surface to transmit. What's more, I'm convinced that there are agents deep inside our command posts. I just don't think that Enigma can be broken. The statistics against it are undeniable, and we're changing settings every damn five minutes of the day, the workload is becoming intolerable."

"There's no need to exaggerate Otto, and yes, I agree with all you say about probabilities and leaks from agents, but the coincidences are just too frequent. What do you think Albert?"

"I disagree profoundly with Admiral Schulz. Statistics are for academics and schoolboys. Anything that can be made by man can be broken by man. Yes, I know that in an ideal world the billions of combinations in Enigma are unfathomable, but men make mistakes and these can be exploited. Look at the double-triple letters that we used for signing in on the early machines. Using them every time enabled the Poles to break them before the war. And the weather forecast area names, repeated day after day in exactly the same order. I know from years of experience in the field that no code is totally secure."

"Well I think also in practical terms," responded Schulz, and in practical terms, with the frequent changes in settings and the larger plugboards, Enigma is practically unbreakable."

General Model had sat in silence through all this and now interjected "So where does all this lead us? What can we do to ensure our communications are secure?"

"Right," said Doenitz. "We tackle the issue on all fronts. As you all know I have already had two in depth reviews of all staff in sensitive positions. We have interviewed all of them and weeded out a few doubtful cases but not found any definite enemy agents. Despite that, we will do it all over again. The Fuhrer has authorised a team of SS officers to assist us.

Secondly, we will add two more rotors to the Enigma spectrum. Thirdly we will audit all operating procedures and training to eliminate slack practices. Finally we will set a little trap for our Allied friends to see if they respond."

"We've already tried that," said Schulz, we sent false rendezvous messages to our U-boats. The enemy destroyers turned up some times, but on other occasions didn't. We still don't know if they got there by chance, by analysing radio traffic or by agent action."

"Well this time, we're going to try something different and you are all going to help. You Schulz with your statistical certainty, and you Praun with your operational experience, are going to work with General Model and I to get to the truth. He will tell you about the new Operations Wacht and Testenwasser.

Model explained "The Fuhrer in the meeting has just this minute authorised my plan 'Wacht am Rhein' for our fight back in Europe. General von Runsted and I have been appointed to lead the attacks so there are going to be some major changes in our deployments. We need to be absolutely sure that nothing leaks out about this at all - it may be our last chance, so we are setting up 'Operation Testerwasser' to ensure absolute security. We will test the water to see if the Allies can read our ciphers."

"In that case, the best way to make a start is to have radio silence," said Schulz. "If we do all communications by landline, at the start of the offensive, then any leaks must come from agents."

"Excellent idea," said Model, "and I'll give you one or two more ideas as well. Please set up a working group and report to me in one week's time." Doenitz concurred and the meeting closed.

Dwight D Eisenhower, Supreme Allied Commander, sat with his SHAEF commanders in the conference room of his chateau in Rheims. After the liberation of Paris he had commandeered, with the reluctant acquiescence of General Charles de Gaulle, the largest chateau which he felt suited his needs.

The subject of his meeting was the strategy for the next Allied moves to defeat Germany. After the failed attempt to strike through to Nijmegen and Arnhem in the operation Market Garden, the Allies had to decide whether to try to secure the approaches to Antwerp or to strike rapidly eastwards and recapture the Rhinelands. There was a belief in some quarters that the German forces would be reeling from the rapid advance from Normandy. General Bernard Montgomery was in favour of a more measured approach but his rival General George Patton favoured the fast and furious approach.

Eisenhower opened the discussion. "Ok guys lets have some ideas here. Omar, what are the options for the Third and Seventh?"

"Strasbourg must be our next objective," replied General Bradley, "if we take it we open up the Saar and then the Rhine is ours."

"Not if, when!" Patton interjected "just give me the gas and the ammo Ike and I'll drive those Kraut bastards all the way to Berlin!"

Eisenhower held up his hand. "Monty, what's your take on it?"

"Not so simple. George is all for a big push, and so am I, but not till we're ready. Every mile we advance to the east lengthens our supply lines, and shortens Jerry's. We need to secure Antwerp and get supplies coming in there. Until we control the Scheldt we still have to rely on the Normandy ports and the supply lines are already overstretched. The 'Montgomery' plan is to use Simonds' First Canadian Army and my Second British to capture Zeebrugge and Walcheren and then when we have a secure supply route, punch our way east into the Ruhr. George's southern proposal is far too long for his supply route already."

Patton spluttered "Not if we build up supplies before we move! I'm sure ...."

Eisenhower intervened, "I like your idea George, but Strasbourg will be no walkover, it's got the high ground and is armed to the teeth. I'm afraid I like Monty's plan to take the Scheldt. The Nazis are raining V2s on Antwerp and every day it's getting worse. It'll take a couple of weeks to get it shipshape again as it is, but if we don't stop them soon we'll be running backwards. We need to chase them out of range of the city and we need that shorter supply route."

"But godammit Ike, that'll take weeks, give 'em time to regroup. We need to go now while they're on the run!"

"Sorry George, but your time will come. Monty, how soon can your planners start?"

"They're already on to it Commander. We'll be ready in a week."

Chapter 25
Uncle Walter

The surprise order came through to Limpet to notify a number of selected Wehrmacht Units in his Sector of an imminent change in Enigma settings. He was told to advise them that one of the wheels was to be changed. This was not, however one of the rotating wheels, but the fixed 'Umkehrwaltze' or 'reflector wheel.'

The Umkehrwalze was a fixed wheel at the extreme left side of the three moving rotors whose purpose was to send the coded signals all the way back through the three rotors to the read-out panel at the top of the machine. The wiring of this wheel was simpler than that of the rotors as it only had one face and the internal wiring just went from one contact to another. The problem for Limpet was that the number of possible wiring arrangements was impossibly high and it would take months to fathom it out.

Back at Bletchley Park the function of the Umkehrwalze was well understood and it was colloquially called the 'Uncle Walter'. There had been three previous versions, known to the Germans as 'A', 'B' and 'C' but referred to at BP as Uncle Albert, Uncle Bob and Uncle Charlie. Albert and Bob had been used by the Wehrmacht and the Luftwaffe, and Charlie by the Navy, and the wiring of all three had been solved by the Polish cryptanalyst Marian Rejewski between 1932 and 1938, long before handing the Enigmas over to the British and French.

Limpet's instructions were to advise his Wehrmacht Units that the new Umkehrwalze would be delivered to the communications centres in late November and would go into service at midnight on the first of December. He realized that he needed to get hold of one of the new wheels as soon as possible, and to advise London of the impending change. The problem was that the Enigmas were made by a manufacturer in Munich and the new wheels would be distributed to the operational units directly by the SS who were entrusted with this sensitive task.

Limpet conferred with Pfeiffer and they sat down and wrote a carefully constructed message. They knew that when they sent it the chances that it would be picked up by a German listening station were high. Limpet would of course, encode the message before transmission but it was not known whether the Nazis had cracked the British code and would be able to read it. If so, the message would have to be unintelligible to the enemy, but understood by London.

Gordon Welchman was sitting at his desk on the ground floor in the Mansion at Bletchley Park when there was a knock on the door. "Come in!"

Nellie Spoforth entered and said "There's a file here for you from Hut Six. Personal delivery."

It was classified 'Top Secret' and sealed with a blob of wax. He mused on this medieval practice as he cracked the seal and opened the file. Nellie, having satisfied herself that the file had been delivered and opened, obtained his signature, excused herself and left.

Welchman perused the single sheet of paper in front of him. It appeared to be a letter home from a soldier. He knew very well that it was from Clam and that it contained a coded message.

'Hello Liebling, I am in good health! We are having a well earned rest after our last battle and I am on two days' leave but I cannot tell you where. I am glad to hear that mother is well and that her brother Richard will start war work at the end of the month. It is a shame that brothers Charlie, Robert and Bert are too old to serve in the war. I will try and let you know how he is getting on. I hope you and Heidi are well. Give her my love. When this war is over we can all be together as before. Much love Liebling, Heinrich.'

Welchman read the message once more then picked up the telephone. "Get me Hut Eight." A short pause. "Alan? Can you spare me a few minutes? Yes, over here. I've something I'd like you to look at."

A few minutes later a lanky ascetic-looking man walked into the room and stood in front of the desk. Welchman said "Have a look at this Alan, what do you make of it?"

Alan Turing read the letter, then read it again. He surmised

"Well, the beginning is just padding, as is the end. The message is in this stuff in the middle, about mother and her brothers."

"Yes, I realise that," said Welchman " but what does it mean?"

Turing mused, "Mother's brother Richard. That's no help I'm afraid, it's Richard in both English and German."

"So Heinrich's mothers' brother, that's his uncle, is Richard. What does that tell us?"

Turing said to himself "And he has three brothers who are too old to be soldiers. Where does that get us?"

Welchman added, "And what's this reference to the end of the month? Are we expecting any new offensives?"

"Not that I'm aware of." Turing was muttering to himself. "let me take this away and think about it." And he left the room with his nose still buried in the words on the piece of paper.

Ten minutes later Turing raced back into Welchman's office shouting "Uncle Richard; Uncle Walter! This is all to do with the Umkehrwalze?"

"I don't see any connection. Where's the link?"

"You see!" shouted Turing "Uncle Richard is Uncle Dick! It's a new mirror wheel!" Clam is telling us there's a new reflector!"

"But I don't see it," said Welchman "what's the rest of the message about?"

"The three brothers who are too old to serve. He's telling us that Uncle Charlie, Uncle Robert, that's Bob, and Uncle Bert, that's Albert, the A, B and C wheels, are no longer in use! The new Umkehrwalze 'D' is coming into use at the end of the month! I'll bet it starts on the first of December!"

Welchman paused, in stunned silence for a moment then slowly said"My god you're right Alan. You've got it. Well done! And well done Limpet and Clam "

179

After a few minutes of mutual congratulations the two cryptographers got down to some serious discussion.

"What are we going to do about it? Limpet hints that he'll try and find out more, but what can we do at this end?"

Welchman was thinking ahead to see if the threat could be anticipated. "What are the chances of us solving the wiring?"

"At the moment, absolutely zero. There are twenty-five times twenty-four times twenty three – all the way down to fourteen times one, ways of wiring that wheel. That is ten to the power of seventeen ways. We can never guess it. We need to get hold of one of the wheels, or get some 'D'-coded messages which we have already decrypted from elsewhere. But if they aren't going to start using it for another fortnight we're stymied."

"It seems as if it's down to Clam to try and get one of the new mirror wheels, and I don't give much for his chances. But let's get a message off anyway"

Chapter 26
Uncle Dick

Limpet waited patiently for the new reflector wheels to be delivered to his department but as the end of November approached he began to realise that it might never happen. After all, the original notification had stated that only certain Units of the Wehrmacht would receive the new Umkehrwalzes.

In his telephone discussions with the army Units in his Sector, he casually asked if they had received the new wheels. None of them had. It seemed as if the security offered by the 'Uncle Dick' wheels was reserved for other Sectors, perhaps for some highly secret operation. He then turned to another tack and found an excuse to call the communications centres of other Sectors. None of them had received the new wheels and by the thirtieth of November it looked as though the idea had been scrapped and he advised London of this.

Then on the first of December a storm of encrypted messages were picked out of the airwaves which could not be decrypted with the Enigmas then in use, which still used the Wehrmacht 'B' Umkehrwalze. Limpet realised that these must be messages encoded with the 'D' wheels and sent to only selected Units. As soon as he got home that night he told Pfeiffer and they sent a message to London explaining the situation and included one of the unfathomable 'D' coded messages.

At BP Alan Turing was looking at a sheaf of thirty-five messages in an undecipherable code. These had been picked up by listening stations all up the east coast of England. They had clearly been encoded with Enigma, and must have been enciphered with the new Uncle Walter 'D' reflector wheel. He looked at the intercept dates and times of the messages and saw that they were all sequential in time, which probably meant that they had been sent out by only one transmitter, one after another.

The Receiving Station's accompanying notes confirmed that the 'touch' and speed of the transmissions suggested just one operator and the Direction Finding showed that they all emanated from a transmitter in the Berlin region. He showed them to his colleague John Tiltman and asked his opinion.

"This seems to have come direct from the German High Command and it suggests to me that there is a new offensive planned or under way and they are using this new code to keep it as secret as possible. Do we have any traffic analysis showing unusual troop movements?"

"Not particularly. Just the usual slight readjustments of the order of battle. Nothing major."

"Let me run these past Hut Six, see if they come up with something. Anything new from Clam?" asked Tiltman.

"Only a message confirming what we already know, and including one of the messages that we already have" replied Turing. "They're still trying to get their hands on one of the wheels."

From some discreet calls to other Sectors Limpet had determined that the newly encoded messages had all originated from Wehrmacht headquarters on the Bendlerstrasse just a few hundred yards from his own communications centre in Berlin. He had visited the headquarters on several previous occasions on legitimate business and found an excuse to do so again. Security at the building was extremely tight but he gained admission without difficulty. He made his way to the coding section and gained admission by showing his papers, which confirmed him as a W/T operator.

Limpet was something of a ladies' man and was soon chatting to one of the female telephonists. He told her that he needed to send a coded message on the department's Enigma machine and was told that he would need to get permission from the Oberfuhrer in charge who was in a security office at the far end of the telegraph room. She also said that he would need to get the Enigma rotors from the safe in the office.

He thought through his options and decided that he would just have to brazen it out. With a thick file in his hand he marched up to the office to address the officer. To his consternation he saw an armed soldier standing guard in front of a large safe in the room. Maintaining his nerve he addressed the officer and said that he had a top secret file which had to remain in the building. He explained that he had to leave the offices for a few minutes but needed to leave the file in the safe. The officer at first demurred but seeing the insistent look on Limpet's face and the large red 'Streng Geheim' label on the file, he agreed. The armed guard stepped aside whilst the officer opened the safe.

Limpet took a packet of cigarettes out of his pocket and offered one to the soldier who happily accepted. A cigarette was then offered to the officer who took it and fumbled in his pocket for a lighter. Meanwhile Limpet had placed the file in the safe and seeing the Enigma rotors on the middle shelf, was momentarily thrown by the fact that one of them was unusually wide. Deducing rapidly that this must be the new rotor, he palmed the fat Umkehrwalze 'D' in his hand. The officer was still lighting his cigarette before offering a light to the guard so Limpet was able to thank them for their help and to say that he would return after fifteen minutes.

As he pocketed the wheel and made his way to the front exit he hoped and prayed that no-one went to the safe whilst he was away. Then he suddenly realised that he was likely to be searched at the doorway, so instead he sought out the men's toilets. Safely inside one of the cubicles he took the wheel out of his pocket and quickly jotted down the sequence of wire connections between the brass contacts onto a piece of lavatory paper.. It took just a minute but he waited another ten minutes before returning to the security office. In the meantime he had wrapped the paper with the connection details in another sheet of paper and concealed it in his cheek. This time when the officer opened the safe Limpet had no difficulty placing the wheel back on the shelf as he picked up his file.

He turned to go and then felt a hand on his shoulder. He started in fear but the officer said "Oberst, thank you for the cigarette. Not many people are so generous in these hard times." Limpet mumbled "Bitte schön" and carefully made his way out of the office. At the exit to the building he was searched but the guard did not look in his mouth.

John Tiltman came into Alan Turing's office and said "I think we may have a crib. One of the encryptions you gave me came in at eleven pm on the thirtieth of November. All thirty-four of the others came in after midnight. The lads have looked closely at the early transmission and it has a peculiarity."

"What's that?" sad Turing "anything we can use?"

"Possibly. The coded message has exactly one hundred letters. It's a bit odd."

"Well, it could just be a coincidence."

"You might think so," said Tiltman, "but there's one other very odd thing about it. There are no letter 'P's in the message, none at all. What are the chances of that?"

"Very slim I should think. Why?"

"The lads think it is a test transmission, but it's very odd." Said Tiltman.

Turing thought a moment. " Yes, let's see. There are twenty six letters on the Enigma machine, no numbers. Assuming the letters are random, the chances of the first one being a 'P' are one in twenty six. No, hang on, as no1 etter can code for itself, the chances are only one in twenty-five. Or rather, more to the point, the chances of it not being a 'P' are twenty four out of twenty five. That's about ninety six percent. The chances of two letters with neither being 'P', using Bayes' theorem, are twenty four over twenty five squared, about ninety two percent, so the chances of a hundred random letters not being a 'P' are point nine six to the hundredth power. That's" – and he thought for a few seconds –"about nought point oh two percent. That's pretty

185

well zero. It's virtually impossible that the sequence comes from a normal text message."

"Yes, that's what the lads in Hut Six are saying. And we know why. The Enigma machine has a weakness. As you say, for all its transformations of letters through the rotors and back, it will never encode a letter as itself. If you type in a 'P' it will never come out as a 'P'. So this means that this message is probably just a hundred letter 'P's. It was a test transmission. What's more, we know something about the operator. He was left-handed. On a German keyboard the letter 'P' is the end key on the left hand side of the bottom row. The lazy idiot just pressed the 'P' a hundred times!"

"That's just brilliant!" said Turing. "But does it help us?"

"It should do. We have the encrypted test transmission and we think it decrypts to a hundred 'P's. We just need to know the rotor settings and the Uncle Walter settings that convert all those 'P's into the code. The lads are running the Bombes now. It could take up to a couple of days but we might get lucky and crack it sooner."

Chapter 27
Churchill and Eisenhower

It took just over forty hours to find the Uncle Walter settings. The Bombes had broken down seven times during the runs. Normally each run would take up to fifteen minutes. To programme the Bombes to cover all the possible combinations of Umkehrwalze wiring required a continuous run of nearly fifty hours and the copper commutator brushes on the many wheels of the Bombe assemblies simply wore out with the friction. It took the delicate fingers of the female Bombe operators to replace and finely adjust the soft new brushes.

However after forty hours and sixteen minutes the almost unbearable buzz in Hut Eleven suddenly broke into an uncanny silence, followed immediately by the shrill bell that announced a possible drop.

The three women in the room froze and then Emily Howerd the shift operator hurried to the end of the rank of Bombes and read off the relay settings. When a possible solution to a crib was found the machine automatically stopped. The time it took to come to a standstill meant that the settings had moved on past the solution values. To overcome this problem, at the instant a solution was detected the values of the settings were sent to a bank of relays and the flags on the appropriate relays would drop.

The term 'drop' came from an earlier era. When the Polish cryptanalyst Henryk Zygalski had first solved the Enigma codes he had done it manually using large sheets of paper with punched holes set out on a grid on each sheet. The sheets were stacked up, over one hundred and fifty of them, and if any of the holes lined up, that represented a possible solution. The test was done with a knitting needle and if it went all the way through, that became the 'drop'.

This Uncle Walter 'D' operation was however much more complicated than the straightforward, if tedious, task of cracking the earlier codes. The process had to be turned on its head. Turing had got the Bombes reconfigured to work effectively in reverse. He reasoned that if he set the first wiring arrangement for Umkehrwalze 'D' at a particular value and then entered a letter 'P', he just had to repeat the setting until the first correctly encoded letter came out. In the intercepted message this was 'S'. The Bombes were set to run at high speed to detect all rotor settings that gave an 'S'. This gave a very large number of possible rotor settings, but by then entering another 'P' he looked for the settings which gave the second intercept letter, 'E'. This resulted in a reduced, but still large number of possible rotor settings.

The process was repeated until five letter 'P's had been entered, by which time the number of possible settings had reduced to only seven. By the time seven 'P's had been entered the possible settings were down to only one. This whole process took only fifty seconds on the Bombe machine. The process had to be repeated for many more possible Uncle Walter wiring arrangements which was why the whole operation took so long.

Emily took the relay readings and then wound the Bombes back the requisite number of revolutions to find the wheel settings and the thirteen pairs of wiring connections for the reflector wheel. She wrote these on a piece of paper and put it into a small container the size of a shoe box. She then put the box on a narrow shute, opened a hatch and pushed it along the shute into the next hut before closing ther hatch again. In Hut Six it was pounced upon by Turing and Tiltman. A technician Nigel Simmonds was standing by and immediately began soldering the wires inside a blank reflector wheel. It took just two or three minutes for him to solder the thirteen wires in place and Tiltman seized it from him, nearly dropping it because the terminals were still red hot.

Turing had an Enigma machine ready and waiting and had already set the rotors and plugboard with the correct settings. Tiltman dropped the Umkehrwalze into its slot and pulled a piece of paper from his pocket. It was the intercept crib from the listening station that had picked it up at eleven pm on the thirtieth of November. With shaking hands he started to enter the five-letter code blocks into the Enigma keyboard.

SEWJF MDOSK JVGLW .....

And the lamp board read out the decrypted message –

PPPPP PPPPP PPPPP .....

Tiltman and Turing leapt for joy. They had done the impossible. They had cracked the wiring of Uncle Walter 'D'.

Tiltman rang Gordon Welchman in his office and gave him the news then went back with Turing to Hut Eleven to congratulate the exhausted girls who had monitored and cared for the Bombe machine during its longest ever run.

They then had to set about the task of deciphering the thirty four intercepted messages from the first of December.

Turing went back to his office and a very agitated Nellie Spoforth was waiting for him. "I'm sorry sir, but I have a top priority Personal Delivery Only file for you. I tried to go into Hut Six but they said you couldn't be disturbed."

"That's alright Nellie, it's been a good day. I don't suppose whatever this is, will top it."

Nellie waited patiently to see him open it.

It was a transcript of a transmission decrypt from Clam.

'Happy to say that our tenacious friends have done well to recover from eating the shellfish. Despite the food poisoning, the Brown Riband meet in Riem was a great success. The odds were, in running order, 13:2; 7:1; 15:3; 22:5; 12:9; 21:8; 11:4; 25:6; 17:10; 16;5; 26:3; 15:12. The rest were out of the running. Good luck next week!'

Turing staggered against his chair and almost fainted. His 'Tenacious Friends' Limpet and Clam had sent him the exact Uncle Walter wiring connections that the Bombes had taken two days to decrypt. Unlike the British who had suspended horse racing since the beginning of the war, Germany continued to hold regular meetings as it was a highly popular sport.

"Are you all right sir?" Nellie asked.

Turing quickly recovered his composture and almost choking, said "Yes, yes, of course. Thank you Nellie." And he signed for the file.

Tiltman and Turing lost no time in starting on the large number of Uncle Walter decrypt and Gordon Welchman lost no time in informing the War Cabinet of the development.

By eight o'clock the following morning over half of the intercepts had been decrypted and forwarded to London by courier. Turing and Tiltman had scoured BP for Enigma machines and seven had been collected in Hut Six. Nigel Simmonds' fingers were raw from soldering up additional reflector wheels for the machines and a team of female typists had been working overnight punching the Enigma keys.

At nine o'clock the Park was presented with some surprise visitors. Overnight General Eisenhower had flown in to Northolt and he and Winston Churchill and the whole War Cabinet arrived at BP in a fleet of government cars. Gordon Welchman met them at the entrance and escorted them to the conference room in Block D.

Churchill asked Welchman for a summary of the decrypts so far.

"The situation is serious. All the messages are orders to a number of Wehrmacht army groups on the Western Front, They are ordered to send troops and weapons to reinforce the existing forces to the east of Metz. Panzer divisions in Belgium are to move to reinforce existing divisions in the Vosges mountains and artillery all along the front are to be moved and concentrated behind Metz. All the indications are that Germany is planning a major counter attack from the Saar sometime before Christmas from the fifteenth of December onwards."

"How long ago were these messages sent?" asked Eisenhower. "Has any activity been reported?"

"The messages were transmitted three days ago early on the first of December. So far there have been no more transmissions; they seem to be maintaining radio silence."

"And troop movements?" persisted Churchill.

"Our reconnaissance shows little by day, and they seem to be well hidden, but we have detected some traffic movement starting just as it gets dark."

A secretary came in with a sheaf of more decrypts. Welchman shuffled through them briefly and said "More of the same. All ordering a build-up of the forces behind Metz."

"How about agents?" asked Eisenhower. Any reports from them back of the lines?"

"Just the usual. Lots of re-adjustments of the order of battle, but nothing major as far as they can see."

"Well we need to increase our reconnaissance. Either the Units haven't arrived yet or they're moving by night and hiding by day. We've just secured Antwerp and the Scheldt and are ready to strike to the Ruhr. The last thing we need is a counter attack on our right flank."

Churchill interposed "Quite right Ike, and we must be prepared for that eventuality. It seems to me that you in SHAEF need to prepare plans for a possible deferment of the Ruhr operation and to redeploy forces further south."

A long debate ensued by the War Cabinet but it concluded with Eisenhower agreeing to put in hand urgent plans to meet the threat. The final redeployment decision would be taken on the eleventh of December. Renewed efforts would be made to obtain more reliable intelligence on enemy troop movements.

The visit concluded with a tour of BP by the visitors who complimented the staff on their work.

Chapter 28
Seeing the Light

All this was unknown to Terry and Limpet. All they knew was that a series of messages had been sent out to a number of unidentifiable Wehrmacht army Units. The decrypts were not known to them and indeed could not be sent to them from London for security reasons. All they knew was that they were receiving frantic requests from London for details of troop and armour movements on the Western Front, and for any W/T transmissions to be forwarded to them.

The two agents sat down and pondered the matter over cups of ersatz coffee. Mrs Hoffman sat in and listened. She was as passionate about defeating the Germans as the two agents. Terry's German network was still intact and he was receiving regular reports from the west. There were no reports of unusual movement. Some re-adjustments were evident at night with one Panzer Unit heading north from the Swiss border, but there was no clear pattern. Radio traffic in the west was very sparse but that from the Eastern Front was as busy as ever as German troops made a slow retreat, some even being sent to the northern end of the Western Front for recuperation.

What more could they do? Terry was pacing up and down, deep in thought. Then he made a suggestion that was not taken seriously at first. "We have the Umkehrwalze 'D' settings, why don't we make one and try some decrypts?"

"It's no use," said Limpet, even with the reflector settings, we still don't have the rotor settings and we don't have a reflector wheel. We'd never be able to do it."

"That's not true," mused Terry. "We have the first of December signals and you yourself sent out the rotor settings to everyone. Did you have to send out different rotor settings to stations with the 'D' Umkehrwalze? Do you have them anywhere?"

"No, I only ever kept them in my memory. With four changes a day since then I just can't remember those for that particular time. And no, as far as I know, none of the Units in my Sector have Umkehrwalze 'D's. If so, they must use the same rotor settings as those Units still with the 'B' version."

"There must be a record somewhere," said Terry. Just because you couldn't write them down to take home doesn't mean there's no record in the office. Who gave them to you?"

"I got them by telephone from Wehrmacht headquarters on the Bendlerstrasse. I wrote them on a piece of paper and after I had transmitted them to the Units my supervisor took it from me."

"The Bendlerstrasse! That makes sense! Said Mrs Hoffman. "That's where you got the Umkehrwalze settings from in the first place! Can you go and get the rotor settings?"

Limpet's face fell. "I don't know if I could. I got away with it last time but I'd be pushing my luck to try again. But I've just had a thought. When my supervisor has a day off, I sometimes take his place. Not always, he rotates it between us operators. But when I was in his office I noticed he is very methodical, very logical. He files everything away. It could be that instead of destroying the settings, he keeps them. I could have a snoop around."

It was far easier than Limpet had hoped. The very next day when his supervisor went to lunch, he went to his office and did a quick search. There were few people about as many had been sent off to one or other front. Those in the office now were very junior to Limpet and asked no questions.

Sure enough, he found what he wanted. Oberstleutnant Eckert was not only methodical, but obsessively so. He had actually had all the information passing through his office typed up and filed, so Limpet's hand-scrawled setting notes were now in a tidy card index. He quickly found those for twelve o'clock am on the first of December and jotted them down. Back in his own office he was now faced with the task of smuggling out an old Umkehrwalze 'A' to take home to reconfigure as an Umkehrwalze 'D'. Whilst this was no longer used it was kept in his office safe to which he had one of only two keys. Security was very tight and everyone was closely searched on entry and exit.

He thought of every possible means to get it past the guards but because the wheel was so large it could not be sufficiently concealed. He realised that he was going to have to re-wire it in the office. This was a possibility because rotors were continually wearing out and requiring new contacts, or wires re-soldered. The problem was that this was usually done by a technician, not a telegraph officer.

Limpet decided to grab the bull by the horns and as he was about to join the other telegraphers to go into Eckert's daily meeting at two o'clock that afternoon, he gave the old wheel and the list of new connections to the technician. He asked him to re-wire it, top priority, top secret. When the meeting was over he collected it from the technician and returned to his desk. He had a pile of routine messages to encrypt and that took him most of the afternoon. He wanted desperately to decode one of the Uncle Dick messages but dared not do so as Eckert kept a constant watch over his team of telegraphers.

As well as being a stickler for record-keeping, Eckert was also a rigid timekeeper and so he went off duty promptly at six pm, even though his staff were still working. He believed the responsibility now lay with the new shift supervisor who, fortunately, was not so prompt in coming on duty. In the five minute gap before he arrived, Limpet had replaced the Umkehrwalze 'B' in his Enigma machine with the new 'D' version, set up the rotors and plugboard to the new start positions and decrypted one of the messages. Not being able to take home a hard copy with him he consigned it to memory, not an easy task as it was quite long. He then returned the Enigma machine to its original settings, locked the Uncle Dick wheel in his safe and went home.

As soon as dinner was over Limpet, his mother Martyna and Terry set to straight away trying to understand the message. Limpet wrote it down as best as he could from memory and they examined it line by line. It was an order to the Sixth Panzer Division in Bonn, ordering them to move half of their forces south forthwith to Strasbourg near the Vosges mountains. It gave detailed dispositions for the deployment of tanks, troops and armour. It also gave orders for the army to come to battle readiness by the fifteenth of December.

Limpet's reaction was to contact London straight away. "I know we've sent them the Uncle Dick connections and they should be able to work the rest out, but what if they can't? Shouldn't we send them this decrypt straight away?"

"I don't think so." said Terry "what if it is intercepted? It'll give the whole game away. We need to think this through. We also need to get some more decrypts. This could be just a minor redeployment. We need to see a fuller picture."

"We haven't got the time. Today's the fifth now. I had one hell of a job getting that decrypt. We can't wait another day to get another."

Terry was adamant. "We may just have to. One more day should give us enough to gauge the picture. Could you do another decrypt during Eckert's lunchtime?"

"Yes but how will I get it to you before the end of my shift? I can't make calls out or stick a bloody red rose in the window or anything."

"Well if we can't do it that way, at least let's get as much information as we can. If you do one at lunchtime and another at six before you come home, we can at least be better informed."

Next evening Limpet was able to do better than that. During lunchtime he had been able to do four decrypts but in the evening the night supervisor arrived on time so another decrypt was out of the question. Limpet couldn't commit to memory all four decrypts word for word, but the gist was very clear. Troops, armour and Panzer divisions were being ordered from all along the Western Front, to converge on the Sector facing Lorraine, with a battle readiness date of the fifteenth of December.

At Eisenhower's daily staff meeting in Rheims the following day, his Senior Planning Officer reported.

"Staff work's almost complete. We're proposing to call it 'Operation Richard' for the redeployment of George and Monty's forces to face the threat to Lorraine. From the thirty-four decrypts, we've a very clear picture of the krauts' Order of Battle and we're countering it division for division, with plenty more divisions in reserve. As far as we can tell, they've no reserves. We'll set in train Operation Richard and attack. We'll bomb their fuel dumps which they have kindly mapped out for us in the Uncle Walter intercepts. We should be able to roll them up in a coupla days. We plan to go a day before them, on the early morning of the fourteenth, catch 'em on the John. All we need is your go-ahead to set it in motion"

"Any more Intel from Berlin?" asked Eisenhower."

"No sir, nor from the kraut radio networks. They're quiet as the grave, must be using landlines only. Complete radio silence. Pretty uncanny. The only movements that Limpet has reported to Clam are some divisions from the Eastern Front being sent to Belgium for rest after their battering by the Russians. Other agents report all quiet too."

"When do you need a decision?"

"Morning of eleventh at the latest. We'll have all the movement orders out tomorrow and we can move very fast once ordered. Two days'll do it. We've not shifted a single soldier yet but Logistics will see it all goes smoothly. Just say the word and we'll get the bandwagon on the road."

"OK," said Ike, "but get me all the Intel you can before eleventh, and try Berlin again."

Meanwhile in Berlin, Terry had made his decision. He was going to have to send a message, and it was going to have to be pretty clear. He would have to take the risk. He and Limpet sat down to try and compose something that might pass muster if intercepted.

The tenth of December came and Eisenhower received his reports at the daily meeting. The staff work had been completed and orders had gone out for the redeployment of Allied forces on the Western Front. The orders for Operation Richard would come into effect at twelve noon the next day when Eisenhower made his final decision. As the meeting was drawing to its close a staff officer came in with a signal. It was from Churchill in the War Cabinet saying that a coded message had been received from the agent in German communications which confirmed the intercepts received from the Umkehrwalze 'D'.

Limpet also put his day to good use and after the usual flurry of sending out encryption codes and then the morning's messages, he had some casual chats with other Units in his Sector. His first conversation was puzzling. He casually asked if the Sector had received orders to redeploy some Panzers and was told not. It seemed strange, because this was one of the Units ordered to send a Division of Panzers to Strasbourg. On reflection, it was also odd that the Unit had not received an Uncle Walter 'D'.

The next conversation was the same. No troops or armour had been redeployed, although the decrypted messages had clearly ordered them to do so. This proved to be the case for two other Units in his Sector, so he called his opposite number in the Strasbourg Sector. No troop build-up was taking place and in fact a Panzer Division had been sent north. Calls to two other Sectors produced similar results.

Limpet had to curtail the calls as his supervisor Eckert was looking at him intently, so he put the telephone down and started encoding some more messages. He went into automatic mode as he thought through the implications of all that he had heard. He could not wait to get home to tell Terry about this strange state of affairs. Six o'clock came and he managed one more decrypt before the night supervisor arrived, but the gist was the same as all the others – redeploy forces to the Lorraine front and prepare to attack.

Over coffee, a substitute made, as far as Mrs Hoffman could tell from tree bark, Terry reviewed with Limpet and Martyna the information that they had gathered. On a scrap of paper he jotted down the facts in chronological order.

1. The Units in all Sectors of the Wehrmacht had been advised of a change to the Umkehrwalze.
2. The new reflector wheel would only be sent to some of the Units.
3. The change of use would come into effect on 1st December.
4. No Sectors or Units appear to have received the new wheels.

5. On 1st December messages had been sent to 34 Units in 7 Sectors of the Wehrmacht.
6. The messages ordered the Units to redeploy forces to the Western Front opposite Lorraine.
7. The messages ordered the Units to be in battle Readiness from 15th December.
8. No such forces had been redeployed.
9. No messages had been sent rescinding the orders.

They read and re-read the list. Suddenly Martyna exclaimed "It's all a bluff! It's meant to get the Allies to weaken their forces along the front!"

"No mama," said Limpet, "they don't know we're reading their messages."

"But what if they do! What if they've found out! They can be using it against us!"

"It doesn't make sense" said Clam. If they knew, they'd change all the codes."

"But they have!" She insisted. "They changed the Umkehrwalze! If the Allies change their troop positions they'll know that we can read their messages and also solve the Umkehrwalze wiring arrangements!"

Terry was stopped dead in his tracks. Realisation dawned. "My God!" he cried. "It's a double bluff! They're finding out if we can crack Enigma, and at the same time using it to send us up a blind alley! Think, think, think! What does it all mean?"

"I'm not with you Clam," said Limpet, "what do you mean?"

"It's all so simple! They are sending messages which none of their Units can receive, so they don't act on them. But if we can read them and move troops to counter the non-existent threat, then they'll know we can read Enigma! They could also use it to make us move forces away from other areas. We've got to report to London before it's too late!"

Chapter 29
Forest Fight

General Eisenhower was in buoyant mood. The Allied intelligence network had provided him with quality information and as a result he was going to pre-empt an enemy counter-attack and break through their defences just when they were expecting to smash the Allied forces. Ike started his routine morning meeting on the eleventh of December 1944 ready to rubber-stamp Operation Richard, his plan to rapidly redeploy his forces to attack the massed enemy which he was told, had assembled in the south of the front, the Saar and Strasbourg area opposite Lorraine.

In Bletchley Park Tinsman and Welchman were struggling to decipher a message that had come in from Clam. Whilst they waited for the arrival of Alan Turing they re-read the terse message from Berlin.

'Dearest Liebling, things are changing rapidly here. We may have to change our plans. I am glad to hear that mother is well, but the news about her brother Richard is worrying. If he's demented it is a very bad condition and likely to produce serious results. It causes delusions. I would not believe a word he says, he must be an inveterate liar. I cannot wait until this war is over, to see you and Heidi again. All my love Liebling, Heintz.'

Turing walked in and Welchman handed him the decrypt. "It's about Uncle Richard again," Turing said. "Uncle Dick. The Uncle Walter 'D'."

"We realise that, but what's all this about being demented?"

"Dementia is all about memory loss. I can't see the significance. Unless he's saying forget everything in the past."

"That could be it. "Tiltman thought a little while. "Do you think that Clam could be saying that the Uncle Dick transcripts are false? Forget all that they are saying? They're all lies?"

"You may be right. We need to get clarification. Can you get a message to Clam and ask him to confirm it somehow?" Welchman shook his head. "It's too late for that. SHAEF are meeting at this very moment and are going to decide whether or not to go. Let's go over it again, what do we know?"

Tiltman summarised; "Uncle Dick is saying that the German army is building up around Strasbourg and planning to attack sometime on or after the Fifteenth. Clam is telling us that no such orders have reached the Units in the field. His contacts are telling him no such concentrations have been observed and our reconnaissance is telling us the same. It looks like a huge bluff. They must know or suspect that we've cracked Enigma."

"Turing said "But why change the Umkehrwalze? That would make it virtually impossible for us to read the messages."

"But we did!" exclaimed Welchman, and if they thought we could, they must suspect that we have a planted agent. This could be a double-bluff, to find out if we can read Enigma and to flush out our agents at the same time."

"It could even be a triple-bluff to direct our forces away from the real area of attack. What do you think? Should we alert the War Cabinet?"

They were all agreed that the Uncle Walter information could be a massive bluff. "I'll get on to Winston right away." said Welchman.

In Rheims it was a fine morning as Eisenhower's Supreme Allied Forces staff assembled for the morning conference. The walls of the elegant salon were hung with opulent drapes of chinoiserie and the high ceilings had elegantly carved plaster cornices intersecting the bleached timber beams dating from the eighteenth century. Most of the drapes however were hidden behind huge maps hung on metal frames, showing the various battle fronts of the war, now entering its sixth year.

Eisenhower first received a report on the ongoing campaign in the south-east of France in the Maritime Alps. Enemy troops were holding out in close-fought skirmishes made extremely difficult by the mountainous terrain.

Next to report was General Mark Clark, commander of Allied forces in Italy who was responsible for the preparation for Operation Grapeshot, intended to end the war in Italy with a spring offensive.

Finally Ike turned his attention to the most important matter at hand, the situation on the Western Front, and asked for intelligence reports. The report was, that there was nothing to report. The situation had not changed and what little intelligence there was came only from the Uncle Walter 'D' intercepts and Clam's apparent endorsement of them.

After some debate the Commander-in-Chief was set to make the decision."Well gentlemen, it looks as if it is 'Go' for Operation Richard. Are we all set?"

"Just say the word Ike" said Patton. "We'll knock'em back to Kingdom Come."

"I cannot but agree" said General Montgomery, "it looks as though we are about to take it to the enemy once and for all and knock them for six."

At a table in a corner of the room a telephone burred quietly. The staff officer at the desk picked it up and listened intently. Putting the receiver on the desk he walked over to Eisenhower and said "The Prime Minister for you sir, urgent."

Eisenhower listened carefully to the call and went back to his seat. "Gentlemen, there appears to be a bit of a new development. The brains at Bletchley are having second thoughts and think there may be a bluff in play. They think that we may be being duped. So, in agreement with the Prime Minister, I am deferring the decision on Operation Richard until six this evening when we should have more Intel."

Patton leapt to his feet "But godammit Ike, we're all ready to go! Put this off now and we won't get the troops in place in time!"

"Six hours won't make that much difference. Winston's putting the Bletchley boys on a plane as we speak. We'll listen to what they have to say. Six pm gentlemen!" and Eisenhower turned on his heel and left the room.

Welchman and Tiltman arrived just after four pm and kicked their heels for two hours until just before the meeting re-convened. Turing had been left at BP to hold the fort and forward any new information. They were ushered into Eisenhower's office and introduced themselves. He thanked them for coming, but also for the work that BP was doing, saying how much it had helped him in planning his campaigns. He listened very closely to what they had to say, nodding his understanding from time to time and asking occasional questions.

The meeting started promptly at six and Eisenhower introduced the two cryptanalysts and asked them to repeat what they had told him. They explained all that they had learnt about the Umkehrwalze decrypts and told of their conclusions. They were then closely grilled by the assembled company on their reasoning. Patton was the most aggressive and challenged on every point. He was clearly just wanting to get on with the job, and concluded his questioning by saying "So all you're telling us, is that this is just a hunch, just guesswork?"

"Not guesswork, a logical deduction based on a high level of probability." responded Welchman defensively

"Deduction! Probability! Poppycock!" growled Patton. Eisenhower thanked the visitors and asked them to leave the room. He polled opinions around the room then said

"I'm pretty convinced. What these guys are telling us makes a lot of sense. We can't afford to deplete the whole of our front line to concentrate on one area if it's a bluff. Our command structure and staffwork is highly flexible, we have the resources and the reserves. If we are wrong and we are attacked in Lorraine, we can quickly execute Operation Richard and move the forces. Then we can counter-attack.

If an attack comes elsewhere, we just change the destination for the Operation. We did have that report about tired Eastern Front troops being moved to Belgium for R and R. What if it's re-grouping, part of a build-up?"

"No way!" shouted Patton. "No way would they want to attack from there. All they have in front of them is thick forest. No, they'll come from Mainz, and we're ready for 'em!"

Montgomery's calm voice intervened. "I wouldn't be so sure about that old boy. That's where they cut through in 1940, simply walking round the top of the Maginot line. Took us completely by surprise. The Jerries still haven't lost their skill with Blitzkrieg. We must prepare for anything."

"Okay," said Eisenhower. "Let's be prudent. We don't want to give away our knowledge about Ultra, but we need to be prepared. Monty, can you move two infantry divisions north, to re-inforce the Belgian front, but do it on the night of the fourteenth, under cover of darkness. Get the planners to work up the alternative options. That's it gentlemen. We sit and wait and listen."

The waiting lasted several days.

The twelfth, thirteenth and fourteenth came and went as tensions mounted in the Allied camp.

At ten pm on the fourteenth Eisenhower put Operation Richard on a two-hour standby, but the fifteenth of December also passed off uneventfully.

At four in the morning on the sixteenth Eisenhower was awakened with a message that activity was being reported in the both the north and south sectors of the front. He convened an emergency meeting of his generals, with Bradley, Montgomery and Patton linked in by secure landlines as they were with their respective armies along the front.

The reports were that attacks were taking place on Allied forces in Belgium, through the Ardennes Forest, and that similar attacks were taking place at Mainz. Bradley and Monty counselled caution, as either could be a feint attack. Patton was more vociferous. "Of course it's a feint in Belgium! The bastards are distracting us so they can start their main thrust in my Sector! You've got to get Operation Richard under way and get the forces down here now!"

Monty was more reflective. "It could be a feint. On the other hand it could be a brilliant stroke. It's typical of Hitler's early successes, before he lost his edge. Remember what I said about 1940, when he dashed around the top of the Maginot Line through Belgium to the Channel ports? If he does the same now he could cut off Antwerp and the Channel ports and cut all our supply lines. We've closed down Normandy, it would take a week to get supplies coming in there again and even then it's a long haul to the front. I say wait. We have the time and resources and have laid plans to quickly redeploy if the Ardennes are the real target."

Eisenhower decided to wait and by eight o'clock the following morning it became clear that there was a major offensive under way in the Ardennes. Panzers of 4 Group had been positively identified in Belgium and it was obvious that the German 'Wacht am Rhein' (Protect the Rhine) operation had begun. The attacks around Mainz were petering out and no strong forces could be identified from aerial reconnaissance.

Eisenhower's planners swiftly recast Operation Richard to redirect forces north but it took a further three days before the battle was joined in full by which time the Wehrmacht had forced the Allies back and created a huge bulge in their line.

At the tactical meeting that morning Eisenhower asked for a report on both German and Allied supplies. The Logistics Officer gave his opinion. "The Krauts are advancing so fast that they are outreaching their landline comms and are having to transmit in cipher. Fortunately they are using the original Uncle Walter 'B' and BP are reading them. The interesting thing is that they are ordering the frontline troops to concentrate on capturing our fuel dumps. They must be scared of running out of fuel. We know the destruction of their refineries and oil wells in Germany and Romania have left then critically short, so this is a desperate last-ditch attempt to win the war. We on the other hand have plenty of fuel but some of our dumps have already been captured.

I recommend that we make a controlled strategic withdrawal to extend their lines and that we destroy any fuel dumps as we go, if we have to. That way we'ill stretch their supply lines and run them out of gas."

What he heard gave Eisenhower reassurance as he addressed the assembled staff officers.

"We have the major advantage, plenty of gas and food, and of course, our divisions outnumber them several times over.

It is only a matter of time, but only if we act clever. What we will do, is let them advance a few miles further, then do a pincer attack north and south on their flanks. If they think they can repeat the Maginot outflanking, we will repeat the Falaise Pocket cut-off."

A few months earlier, as the Allies broke out of Normandy, they had trapped tens of thousands of German troops and armour around the ancient city of Falaise in a classic pincer movement.

And so a few days later the planned counter-attack began. Montgomery's armies attacked the northern flank of the Bulge and Eisenhower asked Patton how soon he could reach the southern flank with his Third Army. He did not believe Patton when he said it would take less than two days, but Patton had already started the planning and put the preliminary moves in hand.

Despite the element of surprise and the highly concentrated forces of the Wehrmacht, their limited supplies of fuel and ammunition meant that it was only a matter of time before the Allies prevailed, although the Germans did manage to extend their range by capturing one or two Allied fuel stores before they could be destroyed.

A crucial point was reached when the town of Bastogne had been cut off by German forces. Patton's armies forced a way up through a fiercely defended road and relieved the town on Boxing Day.

It took until the end of January 1945 for the Wehrmacht to be forced back to its starting point. The bulk of the action had been with the American forces so General Patton got his long sought-after victory, and the end of the war was in sight. The decision to delay the start of Operation Richard did enable the Allies to respond more rapidly to the Ardennes offensive and the roles of Clam, Limpet and the BP team on this were fully recognised.

Chapter 30
Endgame

Testerwasser was regarded by the German intelligence chiefs as a great success despite the defeat of the Wacht am Rhein campaign. The Fuhrer had placed the blame for the failure squarely on the shoulders of General Model despite the obvious inevitability of the collapse of the Wehrmacht offensive due to dwindling supplies. Model was left kicking his heels amongst the General Staff.

As instigator of the Unkerwalze 'D' 'Testing the Water' Testerwasser operation, Admiral Doenitz was very pleased with its apparent success and called a review meeting with Model, Schulz and Praun. He asked each to report on their own areas of expertise.

"General Model, was the 'Testerwasser' operation deception, in your view, successful in terms of deployment of your troops and those of the enemy?"

"Yes, we seemed to have achieved complete surprise. The transfer of infantry and Panzer divisions to the Ardennes was carried out at night and all equipment and personnel were hidden or camouflaged during the day. With control of large parts of the air over the front the Allies carried our many daytime reconnaissance sweeps but didn't seem to detect our movements."

"Good", enthused Doenitz, "that is good! But did the Allies move any of their forces?"

"There was no reinforcement of the Allied front in Belgium prior to the attack. In addition there was no reinforcement of the front opposite Metz so our strategy seems to have worked. It is impossible that they could have read the transmissions sent using Umkehrwalze 'D' otherwise they would certainly have responded. For the same reason they could not have been getting information from agents. The only thing that did surprise me a little was when they started destroying their fuel dumps in the Ardennes. It did make life very difficult for us."

"A minor matter", said Doenitz, "We were always going to run out of fuel sooner or later. Now Praun, what about communications?"

"Full radio silence was observed for the first three days of the advance. Only landlines were used to send orders to the front line troops and back. The fluidity of the situation after three days was such that landlines could not be laid quickly enough but by then the Allies were fully aware of the scale of the offensive and so there was no point in not using W/T. I think I can say that we fully acquitted ourselves on the communications side."

"Yes General Praun," said Doenitz, "congratulations on an excellent operation. But what happened with operational procedures? What changes were made?"

"I introduced a crash programme of re-training and changed many of the procedures used for setting up and enciphering messages. The number of sloppy practices that had developed is unbelievable. I personally visited many command centres and made examples of a few of the worst offenders. They are cooling their heels in the icy marshes of the Eastern Front as we speak."

"That is good Praun, good. And Schulz, what do you make of the outcome?"

"Just as I'd said all along," sneered Schulz," Enigma is to all intents and purposes unbreakable. All this complication of producing a one-off Umkehrwalze just to send false information was a complete waste of time. Weeks of valuable intelligence resource were expended for no good reason, just to find out what I already knew."

"You may be right General Schulz, but we now have certainty. We can stand down much of our security around Enigma for the present. In fact it will be necessary to do so. Our reserves and resources are much depleted by the setback of Wacht am Rhein and we're having to redirect many administrative staff to the front. The Allies are bound to counter attack at any moment and we're rebuilding our divisions as quickly as we can. The Fuhrer has lowered the age of conscription and we're recruiting young men of fourteen. He has also ordered that older men who had retired with minor war wounds should be re-enlisted."

Praun interjected. "Is that wise? I still disagree with Schulz about the codes being unbreakable. We can't be sure that the Allied codebreakers weren't just too slow to do so in time. The new Umkehrwalze might have just prevented them. It could take weeks to find out the wiring. We might have just been too clever."

Doenitz did not agree. "I'm told that if they have the details of the rotors and plugboards, then it would be much easier to work out the Umkehrwalze wiring. The fact that they didn't seems conclusive to me that we are secure."

If Doenitz felt secure, then Limpet and Terry certainly did not. The 1945 winter turned to spring and the Allies made rapid advances on both main fronts. Limpet's office in Berlin became increasingly perilous as the Russians ground their way across eastern Germany towards the capital.

Terry was equally uncomfortable. He was still conducting his network activity from the apartment he shared with Limpet and Martyna but it necessitated regular trips out to various rendezvous in the city. Travelling amongst the emaciated citizens of a crumbling Berlin he attracted many strange looks and comments from people on the streets. There were few men about and those were often clearly maimed with missing arms or legs. Terry's almost fully reconstructed face gave him at first glance the appearance of a perfectly healthy man.

It was the women mainly who accosted him and accused him of being disloyal, so he avoided daytime travel whenever he could. As a retired war veteran he had taken on a daytime job loading high explosive into shells in a factory on the west side of the city and he went to work and returned home in darkness. Security at the factory had deteriorated as guards were taken away to serve on the front so Terry was able to secrete a small amount of explosive in a false pocket in his trousers each day and take it away for his sabotage networks.

One day in March as he was leaving he was directed by a guard to a small office where two Wehrmacht officers were sitting. He feared that he was about to be searched but was relieved when instead they quizzed him about his war record and his wounds. Pfeiffer knew that his papers as a retired veteran would not stand examination so relaxed a little when they were given just a cursory glance and returned to him. Then came the bombshell.

"Oberst, it is clear that you are a very brave man and that you have suffered very much for the Fatherland. But now the Fatherland is suffering for you and needs your help again. In view of your excellent recovery from your wounds you are being returned to active duty. I know that you will serve the Fuhrer well and you are to report tomorrow morning at the Wehrmacht offices in the Tiergarten at nine am."

Terry duly reported for duty and was assigned to a Panzer Division in Hamburg. He was given a rail warrant and told to depart immediately.

Worse was to come for Limpet. Two weeks after Pfeiffer had left, his section in the command centre was dissolved and the soldiers given warrants to join troops in the war zones. He was sent to the Russian front where he joined an infantry brigade which was fighting a rearguard action trying to defend East Berlin. He had an emotional parting with his mother who was left on her own in the apartment, living on her meagre pension. He promised to send money home from his pay, but ten days later Martyna was visited by an apologetic officer who told her that he had been reported missing, presumed dead. He did not tell her that fragments of Limpet's unrecognisable body had been found on the edge of a shell crater and only his dog-tags enabled him to be identified; 'Oberst Dietmar Hoffman.'

Terry, in the guise of Kurt Pfeiffer, arrived at the 106 Panzer Brigade headquarters east of Hamburg just as a failed offensive against Allied troops had ended. He was sent immediately to retrieve and repair damaged tanks from behind the new lines. His initial problem was that despite being a supposed Panzer driver, he knew little about it. Fortunately he was able to explain that, not only had he driven much earlier models, but that his head injuries had caused partial loss of memory. He was given another driver to teach him the basics of the Tiger II and soon learnt sufficient to pass muster. As nearly all the Panzer crews were virtual novices, most of them aged between fifteen and twenty, his erratic driving was not out of the ordinary.

Terry had but one objective; to get back behind Allied lines. He thought that it would be relatively straightforward. His plan was that on the next offensive he would stall his tank when the inevitable retreat was sounded, wait until the rest of his Panzer group had gone and then surrender to the Allied troops as they advanced. It didn't turn out that simple. When he stalled the tank his captain, Hauptmann Standl, cursed him and ordered him to restart immediately. As he fumbled with the controls the Hauptmann drew his pistol and ordered Terry to get out of the driving seat. He then took over the steering himself and drove the tank back over behind the German lines.

With the crew out of the tank the Hauptmann accused Terry of cowardice and threatened to shoot him. Terry pleaded that in the heat of the battle he had got confused with the controls and was still not conversant with this latest Tiger model which had only been in service for a few weeks. His explanation was grudgingly accepted but the captain made it very clear that he would be watching him closely.

Standl's determination was brought home during the next offensive, this time by the Allies. The Panzer group went into counter attack but the slow Tiger with its heavy armour and huge 88mm gun was no match for the agile Comet tanks of the Armoured Brigade of the Second British Army. With shells and arms fire bouncing off the armoured sides of the Panzer, the inevitable radio signal to retreat was received and this time Standl stood over Terry with his pistol drawn.

The Panzer gunner was standing in the turret with the hatch open and suddenly started to climb out. Standl cursed and climbed after him. Just as his head came out of the hatch he saw the gunner dive over the side and start running towards some bushes. Standl took aim and shot him cleanly through the head.

Terry realised that escape was not going to be so easy as he had thought. Just as he was musing on this Standl fell backwards down into the tank with half of his face shot away, and lay twitching over a stack of 88mm shells. Terry stopped the Panzer and he and the other three crew members climbed out and scattered. Moments later a direct hit underneath the turret blew it high into the air. Shrapnel fell everywhere and a huge fragment hit Terry in the stomach causing a large excruciating wound.

He was picked up by a British stretcher party a few minutes later and taken to a field hospital. His recollection of the next few days was non-existent and his first memory was waking up with a vast stab of pain in his belly as a nurse removed the dressing. She told him in halting German that the wound was healing well and he had been treated with a new wonder drug Penicillin which miraculously killed off any infection. She told him that he was in a field hospital for seriously wounded German patients and that his army had just surrendered to General Montgomery. He also learned that Hitler had killed himself and Admiral Doenitz had assumed the role of Chancellor of Germany.

Terry realised with a flash of memory that as far as the hospital was concerned, his dog tags said that he was a German Panzer driver and he asked to speak to an officer. She told him that a doctor would be round to see him later in the morning. He tried to explain that he was English but she just assumed he was delirious.

He told the German-speaking English doctor when he arrived that his name was Terry Sexton and that he was a British Lieutenant on a special mission and needed to speak to an army officer immediately. The doctor was dubious but confused by Terry's perfect English. He asked him a few questions about the English way of life and was soon convinced that Terry was either genuine or a very well schooled German agent.

An hour later a Colonel of British Intelligence arrived and quizzed him. Terry gave the officer a telephone number to call in London to verify his identity. It took many hours for the matter to be cleared up but Terry's scarred face was sufficient to convince those in London and Germany that he was genuinely who he said he was.

Terry was still completely immobile and was moved to a hospital in Paris for British officers where he would have to stay until he was fit enough to be flown home. On the evening of his first day there, a surprise visitor strode into the ward and stood with his hands behind his back to address the dozen or so officers. Wearing his distinctive beret and battle dress bespangled with medals, he announced-

"I don't know you chaps, but you know me. It's not often that I can get to visit a hospital for the wounded. I haven't had the time. Now I seem to have a little more time on my hands.

Death and injury are an inevitable part of war, a fact that I have had to take in my stride. You chaps are the lucky ones. Better you lying wounded in here with excellent nursing care and the enemy lying dead outside, than the other way round. You and men like you, have resoundedly beaten the enemy.

Three days ago on Luneburg Heath I took the surrender of all enemy forces in Denmark and North-West Germany. General Patton was still fighting in the south. I have just come from the offices of SHAEF in Rheims, where this afternoon General Eisenhower took the general surrender of all German forces, on the continent of Europe and overseas. This is a marvellous and well earned victory. Well done! Now for Japan. Thank you all. God Save the King!" Montgomery turned briskly on his heel and strutted out into the next ward where he repeated his address.

It took some time for Terry to catch up with all the news about the end of the war and the suicide of Hitler. Churchill's great ally Franklin Roosevelt was always suspicious of Britain's colonial aspirations and during discussions in Yalta in February 1945 with Churchill and

Stalin, the post-war spheres of influence were discussed. Churchill was keenly aware that the United Kingdom had gone to war to protect Poland but Roosevelt did not see this as a priority. With the end of the war in sight his eyes were already turning to the Pacific war. He wanted to see the European war concluded as soon as possible so that he could concentrate on fighting Japan and then 'bring the boys home'. Thus when Stalin lobbied hard for Poland to be in the Soviet sphere of influence and promising free elections, Roosevelt agreed, despite Churchill's objections.

After Roosevelt's death Harry Truman had been sworn in as the new President. He shared his predecessor's views and his main concern was his struggle over the decision to use the atomic bomb in Japan. Then when Churchill lost a General Election in July 1945 and Clement Attlee became Prime Minister with a programme of major domestic reform, Poland became even less of a priority. Terry learnt about the Allied division of Germany into Sectors occupied by the different countries, but was most concerned about Poland which now lay totally under communist rule. He worried about all his friends who had fought so hard for their freedom.

Terry stayed another two weeks in Paris before being flown home in a C47 Dakota with half a dozen other wounded officers. He was whisked off to a former sanatorium at Harefield which had been converted to a hospital for thoracic and abdominal surgery. He shared a cubicle with a young fighter pilot who had just had a lung removed.

The hospital was very convenient for Amersham and on the first day Vivien came to see him with Sarah and their new baby Helen. He was overcome with emotion when he saw them all and fell in love with Helen straight away.

Before they left he asked after Rich and Vivien said "He's alright at the moment but with the end of the war, there's talk of layoffs because they don't need the aircraft now. He's been working on the new jet bombers but it's already slowing down. He's going out with a girl from Handley Page. She seems very nice. Actually, Rich would really like to come and see you. Can you face that?"

"Yes, of course. I really want to see him too. It's been a long time. Tell him it'll be all right."

Terry had a stream of visitors over the next few days. First came Freddie Younge, who had taken over Sir Cedric Attenby's post. Sir Cedric apparently had retired and been made a member of the House of Lords.
"So as soon as I get out of here," said Terry, "it's back to Poland I suppose, start all over again behind Russian lines."

"Not for you old boy, I'm afraid. We've already got someone on to it. It's honourable retirement for you now. Your face is literally, too well known."

Next came Lord Attenby of Uxbridge himself, wrapped in the usual cloud of cigar smoke. He was immediately torn off a strip by a nurse who couldn't have been more than eighteen but she told him in no uncertain words that this was a ward with chest surgery patients and smoking was strictly forbidden.

Lord Attenby was immensely proud of himself and told Terry that his elevation to the peerage was due to the role his department had played in not depleting the forces in the Ardennes.

"Bit of a rum deal really, rewarded for saying 'stay put.' More down to you and Limpet really," he said, "like the OBE, Other Buggers' Efforts."

Rich came to see Terry soon afterwards and they were soon chatting away together about old times. When it was time for Rich to leave he said "I know it's an imposition. But would you object if I came to see you all from time to time/"

"Of course not Rich. In fact Vivien and I would like you to be Helen's godfather if that's alright with you?"

It was another seven weeks before Terry was allowed home and he returned to Amersham feeling as fit as he ever had been. His ox-like constitution had stood him in good stead.

With his military career at an end he searched around for something to do. He decided to retrain for a new career and the disability lump sum and pension he received was used to take a course in surveying which would build on his earlier experience in the construction trade.

In 1947 Terry went to Berlin to try and find Martyna Hoffman. He could not even find the street, although he knew it had to be in the British Sector. The whole area had been flattened during the final advance by the Russian army. He made inquiries at the Deutsches Rotes Kreuz tracing service, the German Red Cross, but they had no records of people living in many parts of Berlin during the war. He tried to make contact in Poland to find any remaining relatives but drew a blank from the Soviet authorities. He had to accept the fact that her part in helping to end the war in Europe would go unrecorded.

Epilogue

For the next thirty five years Terry Sexton earned his living working for large and small civil engineering contractors. He and Vivien raised their girls to be two lovely young women who in turn presented them with grand-children. Rich stayed on with Handley Page and worked on one of the new generation of V-bombers, the Victor. He was a friend into old age with the Sextons.

Terry made several attempts to contact friends in Poland, to little avail. On a holiday to Rhodesia he and Vivien were able to track down Sylwia Zawadzka, formerly Baranska. Sadly they learnt that her fiancé Bill Dawson had been shot down over Hungary whilst on a bombing raid in August 1944. All she had was a cigarette case that had been sent to her following his death.

After General Franco died in 1975 Terry and Vivien went on holiday to Spain and he was able to locate some of his friends from the Civil War days. He also re-acquainted himself with Veterano and had a very convivial time recalling the old exploits. A year later Terry and Vivien returned to Spain and bought a villa near Alicante. Sarah and her family eventually bought a permanent home in the hills behind Alicante.

In 1996 Vivien died and Terry scattered her ashes in a little stream in Amersham near where they used to walk. Terry continued to spend most of his time in Spain where he had a large circle of Spanish and ex-patriate friends. Gradually his health deteriorated so he reluctantly sold the villa and moved back to the house in Amersham. When he could no longer cope with the house he sold it and moved in with Helen who was living in a Cotswold village.

He joined in the village life in full, being a regular in the pub, but still liking to drink Veterano at home, with which he was regularly supplied from Helen's frequent visits to Sarah in Spain. Terry was a member of the Royal Antediluvian Order of the Buffaloes, 'The Buffs', in the village and only latterly would he talk about his wartime experiences. However he always wore his medals proudly at the annual Memorial Service.

For his eighty-fifth birthday a friend of Helen's took him for a flight in his small two-seater Cessna and he was able to enjoy the beautiful sight of the Cotswolds from the air on the bright summer's day. It was in stark contrast to his terrifying night flights during the war. On landing they went to the Control Tower and he was introduced to the controller Chris who asked in a very patronising manner "Have you ever flown in a light aircraft before, Terry?" Terry replied laconically "The last time I was in a light aircraft I was baling out of a burning Lysander over France."

After his death in 2010 aged eighty-nine, Terry's ashes were scattered in a garden of remembrance. Sarah came over from her home in Spain for the funeral. The wake was held in Helen's house and when the last ofl the mourners had left, the two sisters started sorting out Terry's possessions and letters. As well as family letters, stamp albums, a 1944 German First Day Cover showing beautiful racehorses, and two Polish medals, they found a tattered copy of another letter :-

321 Townsend Road
Chesham
Buckinghamshire

4th April 1946

Mr Douglas Jay
Private Secretary to the Prime Minister

Dear Mr Jay,

Thank you for your letter of 2nd April advising me that the Prime Minister is minded to recommend my name to His Majesty the King for the award of an Honour.

After much reflection I have decided to decline this offer.

I feel however that I owe the Prime Minister an explanation.

Before the War I made many Polish friends, both in Eastern Europe and during the Spanish Civil War. Great Britain went to War with Germany in September 1939 in defence of the solemn treaty we had made with Poland to come to her aid. I was asked and proud to serve His Majesty's Government in assisting with the war effort in Poland, France and Italy.

In July 1943, the day before his death, General Wladyslaw Sikorski bestowed upon me the highest Polish military honour, the Virtuti Militari. In November of that year the Polish Prime Minister in Exile Stanislaw Mikolajczyk awarded me the Polonia Restituta, the highest civil award for service towards the restoration of a free democratic government to Poland.

I was dismayed therefore when I learnt that at the Fourth Moscow Conference the then Prime Minister Winston Churchill had relinquished Poland to Russian communist control, and further appalled when the present Prime Minister endorsed this at the Potsdam Conference.

It is therefore with no regrets that I decline this offer of the British Government and content myself with the honours bestowed upon me by my Polish friends.

Yours faithfully,

Terence Patrick Sexton, VM PR

Also by Will Fenn

Fifty Shades of Yarg   ISBN 978-0-9554455-9-0
History of cheesemaking and recipes.

and by William Fairney

The Knife and Fork Man   ISBN 978-0-9554455-2-1
The Life and Works of Charles Redrup (2nd Edition)

Richard Stephens and the Clevedon Motor Cars
              ISBN 978-0-9554455-4-5

The Engineering Design Manual for Lead Balloons
              ISBN 978-0-9554455-8-3

Just my Doggerel   ISBN 978-0-9554455-1-4
An anthology of the Writings of Joseph Johnson Fairney

The Higgs Way to weight Loss (Kindle only)
              ISBN 978-0-9554455-6-9

The Bristol Treasure Island Trail
Jointly with Mark Steeds   ISBN 978-0-9554455-3-8

www.dieselpublishing.co.uk   dieselpublishing@gmail.com

Printed in Poland
by Amazon Fulfillment
Poland Sp. z o.o., Wrocław